I0746255

Blood
in the
Shadows

A LEGACY NOVEL

Allyson Lindt

For my eternal dragon

PROLOGUE

12 YEARS AGO
STARKAD

Starkad studied the photo on his desk. The girl who stared back was young, but it was Kirby. The reincarnation of the Valkyrie he'd loved nearly two thousand years ago. He'd lost track of how many times she'd been reborn. They'd never found her before she hit her twenties. Why this time?

He had two calls to make. He dialed Min, and was both disappointed and relieved to hear, "Where is she?"

"Hang on. Getting Gwydion on the line." Starkad didn't agree with a lot of technology, but a three-way conference call was far more convenient than carrier pigeon or Pony Express. He dialed Gwydion next.

"It's only been fifteen years," Gwydion answered.

Starkad smiled dryly at his empty office. It was the only reason he'd call. "She's here. She's part of the program. And she's thirteen."

Here was a school and training facility for The Order of Mistletoe. A series of prophecies had been written thousands of years ago, about the destruction of several gods, and the birth of new gods who would replace them. TOM had been created by a number of the gods whose names sat under the *To Be Terminated* column. Starkad taught at a campus where they trained assassins to eliminate the threats—people who had the potential to become new gods, and replace the old.

Starkad didn't support their cause. He was here as a double agent, sharing his knowledge with the Followers of Urd, and he'd been in for a long time.

"Great. Where can I meet you? How soon until you can pull her?" Gwydion asked.

Starkad loathed the program here. He'd never expected this part of his past to be enrolled in it. Then again, she was drawn to war in every life. As a Valkyrie, the impulse was embedded so deeply in her, it came as naturally as breathing. And in this modern world, wars were comprised of subterfuge and terrorism.

And Kirby would be safer here than on any battlefield. "You misunderstand. She's not going anywhere."

"Bullshit." Gwydion snapped the word off. "They'll turn her into a killer baby. And then a baby killer."

"They'll teach her to defend herself. In these walls, she stays alive." Starkad could keep an eye on her from a close distance. She'd learn the skills she needed to survive.

Gwydion's low growl was expected. "Send her to Switzerland. Or Australia. Put guards on her. Give her a real education, not a brainwashing."

Starkad scrubbed his face. "Last time you found her, she had her memory and wings for more than a year before she was killed. We don't know what will keep her safe. But at least in this place, she'll learn to defend herself. Besides"—he hated to play this card, because it felt manipulative. It was also true—"you take her now, and that's grooming a child to love you. That's fucked up. It doesn't matter who she becomes; it's not who she is yet."

"And how is TOM going to be any different?" Gwydion asked.

"I'm not preparing her to fall in love before she even understands the concept."

"No. You're letting them train her to kill before she solidifies her own moral existence."

For Starkad, his entire life had followed a trail of death. He was a berserker. He'd fought side by side with Odin's other fiercest warriors. Even as civilizations moved away from blatant brutality, it still ran through humanity's veins. He'd witnessed it over and over.

So had Kirby. And she would continue to do so for eternity. However, Starkad understood that the world no longer liked to admit people thought that way. Showing Kirby that truth from the start of life would change her perspective.

Decisions had to be made though. "Death is part of our world. She's a Valkyrie. Taking lives is literally what she does."

"No." Gwydion had always struggled with Kirby's origins. "She's not a Valkyrie yet, any more than she's your Ruby."

The name sliced through Starkad like a rusty blade. "Do you have a better idea? How are you going to keep her safe if you take her? How will you teach her to defend herself from the world? Not the mortal one. One filled with gods who want her and others dead."

"I don't know." Defeat rang heavy in Gwydion's reply.

"Having no plan is worse than having a shitty plan."

"Not in this case."

"Min. Break the tie," Starkad said. A cruel request, but one that would ensure Starkad got his way.

Gwydion sighed. "Don't—"

"I vote with the berserker." Min was a god of passion. He loathed death. He'd also seen Kirby die too many times to allow things to continue as they always had.

Starkad was both smug and disappointed to get his way. "It's settled. She stays with TOM. She trains. She'll be hidden in plain sight, and she'll learn to protect herself."

"She can't defend herself from a bullet fired from a thousand meters, regardless of how much training you give her." Gwydion sounded defeated.

No. But she'd learn how to be the one firing that bullet, and that would teach her a lot about avoiding the same thing. "If you find us, you can have her." Starkad disconnected.

Things would be different this time. He'd loved Kirby in every life he'd known her, but this girl… She *was* just a child. And he'd do whatever it took, to keep her alive. He'd do the one thing none of them had tried yet.

He'd refuse to love her, even after she became an adult.

CHAPTER ONE

NOW
KIRBY

There were too many places for a sniper to hide here. Too many empty offices, corners, and short buildings with accessible and unguarded rooftops.

And while there weren't nearly as many people as someplace like New York City, Salt Lake was still far too populated for Kirby's comfort.

Just once, she wished The Order of Mistletoe—or TOM—had picked a target who lived by themselves on fifty acres of isolated land. There were too many options for casualties here.

"Do you really think they'll do this in the morning? During peak traffic?" Kirby sipped her coffee, her attention never wavering from their surroundings.

Starkad sat next to her on the bench, arm pressed to hers. He'd be watching the same things she did, through mirrored shades. To everyone else, they looked like one of those star-struck couples who just *had* to sit next to each other.

The reality was so far removed from that, it wasn't funny. Neither of them would sit with their backs to the door or the windows, especially on a mission.

And Starkad had made it painfully clear—he could have written it in neon in the middle of Times Square, and it wouldn't be clearer—that Kirby was a weapon and a tool for him. Nothing more.

"That's what I hear." Starkad broke off a piece of his muffin and popped it in her mouth.

His sources were never wrong. Her ties with TOM had been severed, but he still knew people on the inside.

She used to ask more questions. *Do we know which team they're sending? Which prophecy is about this target? Who's your source? Why are you such a stoically sexy, unyielding prick?*

He never gave her answers, so she stopped trying.

Fortunately, he knew people on the other side, too. The organization funding and supporting Kirby and Starkad's trips was The Followers of Urd—they believed Fate would see her will carried out. Kirby thought that was a lot of bullshit, but they got her closer to accomplishing her goal.

She downed the rest of her coffee and slid him the cup. "Sweetheart, would you get me more?" She poured as much sugar into her request as she'd dumped into her drink. The couple illusion helped them blend in. The more boring and *status quo* they appeared, the better.

"Of course, kitten." He kissed her on the cheek, before heading to the drink station.

This was where the target got coffee every morning before work. Her schedule was as clockwork and reliable as most peoples—as in, ninety-nine percent predictable. She took the train downtown. She stopped at this place, where she got a wholegrain bagel, toasted, with cheddar cheese and tomato, plus decaf coffee. And then she walked across the street to the office building she worked in. The target was on a TOM hit list because she had the potential to ascend to godhood.

Kirby wasn't surprised this individual lived a flavor of the same humdrum life as most people. She wished she could argue that gods were more interesting than the standard mortal. Considering the few who had been involved in her training and upbringing, she knew better. Crueler lives maybe, but not any more fascinating.

She'd already checked the angles from every part of the coffee-shop interior. There were no clear lines of sight into the building from anyplace outside, except the TRAX station in the middle of the street. TOM wouldn't attack from there. There were too many people in the way, to ensure a clear shot.

Kirby would use Starkad's opinion to make sure she hadn't missed anything. Not that she ever did.

As Starkad walked away, she took the opportunity to appreciate the view. He was an asshole, but he made for some good scenery. At almost six-foot-three, he towered over most people.

His shoulders were so broad, sometimes it was tempting to hang off those arms.

Her ass knew firsthand what kind of power was in those biceps. The memory of the art he created with a cane on her skin made her squirm.

His dirty blond hair was just long enough to muss—it had to look like everyone else's—framing a strong jaw decorated with a few days' worth of dark blond scruff. And he had ice-blue eyes she swore could see more about her soul than she would ever understand.

He'd also saved her life a few years ago, and aside from the refusing-to-fuck-her thing, had never steered her wrong.

It was probably for the best. He was a teacher when she entered the academy at thirteen, so he had to be at least twelve years older than she was. Not that it showed in his face or movements, but that made him almost forty now. At least.

The last thing she needed was to get hung up on some Daddy fantasy.

Too late.

Starkad returned but didn't sit. He handed her the paper coffee cup. "They're out of honey."

"Aww." She pouted, stood, and took the drink. This place didn't have honey, and she didn't drink it in her coffee.

His comment meant he didn't see anything worth worrying about either. It wasn't so much an established code phrase, as an off-the-cuff, *this doesn't matter—let's go.*

They stepped outside, merging into morning foot traffic and letting it carry them back toward their hotel. "I'm liking the look of those office buildings." She nodded to the ones next door to the coffee shop. "How long do you think they'll be remodeling?"

"Another month or so. The timing should be perfect."

She agreed.

They shifted from small talk laced with hidden meaning to plain, old, boring small talk. It was meaningless, and intended for anyone eavesdropping, rather than for the two of them.

Kirby let her mind wander. She'd like to say she'd lost track of how many of these jobs she'd done, but she remembered every one of them.

Eight hunts. Sixteen executions. Thirty-two eyes of former classmates that she'd looked into, before pulling the trigger.

It was almost the stuff of fairy tales. The dark kind that went terribly wrong, leaving the reader wondering where the moral was.

She wished she could forget some of it, but with each job, it all rushed back, as if she'd lived it yesterday.

She had been the thirteen year-old orphan who was more trouble than she was worth. When TOM found her, she was promised glory and the ability to stick up for the little guy.

The reality was darker—an institute where children were trained as hunters and assassins. Their sole goal was to destroy potential gods, before the individuals ascended and brought destruction and ruin to the world.

At least, TOM spun them as being destructive forces. Turned out, potentials were competition, and the gods who'd created TOM were unwilling to share the spotlight. It might literally destroy them.

If Kirby hadn't believed in the gods before she got there, she definitely did after seeing what they could do. Thanks to that knowledge, and the way they'd cast her aside like so much garbage, she'd made her mission to help speed along the demise of the gods who ran TOM.

She had been their top student. Ace sniper. Fighter. Top honors in every class.

And when she was betrayed, expelled, and nearly died, she discovered what they really were— a group of petty gods, looking to bring about Ragnarok.

She was a real life Deadpool, except without the super healing to back up the years of torture and psychological abuse.

And just like Wade Wilson, she was tracking down the people who did this to her, to make things right.

Fortunately, Starkad knew people. An entire organization of immortals who were fighting to make sure the gods that ran TOM didn't take out all of humanity in their own bid to survive. He used those connections, plus a contact on the inside at TOM, to point himself and Kirby toward planned assassinations. Kirby hunted the hunters and killed them before they could take lives—innocent or potentially godly—now or ever again. She stopped the TOMs and was rapidly diminishing their numbers.

They reached their hotel. She drew a small amount of amusement from the fact it was across the street from a temple that didn't belong to any god involved in this whole fucked-up mess.

They slept in separate rooms when they traveled. It marred the illusion of the happy vacationing couple, but Starkad insisted, since their… blowout a few years back. She assumed he went out and got laid. She did. School taught that sex was stress relief, and she knew how to stay removed. Sex was also the only time she allowed herself to surrender control.

But tonight, she'd be in his room, finalizing tomorrow's plans. They'd sleep during the day. Waking up hours before the hunt would give her time to shake off any drowsiness and ensure she was alert.

Back in her room, she hung out the *do not disturb* sign, drew the blinds as tight as she could, popped a couple of Ambien, and let the pills drag her into sleep.

She tossed and turned for the next ten hours—as was typical the day before a hunt. She was about to look former classmates in the eye and execute them for doing the only thing they'd ever known.

The first time she'd done it, she stayed at a distance. Her specialty was sniping, and she took out her target from a few thousand meters, watching them through a scope. It should have been easier that way. Less personal. She didn't sleep for weeks after.

Doing the job in person let her apologize. It was closure. They never begged for mercy, or made promises to change if she just let them go. They'd all be trained too well for that. But face-to-face felt more like real combat. Maybe it would still give her former classmates their time in Valhalla

When it was time to get up, she struggled to wake up. The cold shower helped a little. The coffee helped more. This would get her through planning. The Adderall she would take before they set up, combined with a heavy dose of natural adrenaline, would keep her sharp when the time came.

She dressed in worn, baggy clothes. She and Starkad didn't want to be the cute couple for this stage. They'd look destitute—the kind of down on their luck that most people turned away from. The oversized clothes would mask their appearance, and the backpacks would hide their weapons.

Kirby's shoes didn't make a sound on the carpet as she strolled down the few doors to Starkad's room.

He still answered before she knocked. He would have spotted her shadow under the door and seen her through the peephole as she approached.

He had set up his computer on the table in the corner, and white noise filtered from the speakers.

Kirby gave him a grateful smile when he handed her another cup of coffee. She should buy stock in Folgers, give herself a nest egg of her own money to retire on—she drank so much of the stuff.

She took a long sip of the almost too-hot drink and let it sear through her veins, before saying, "Thanks. And hi."

"Hello." He nodded toward the equipment. "The rest of the blueprints and realtor information came in today."

"Cool." She dropped into a seat, and he did the same. They got such short notice about new jobs, it was always a scramble to gather sufficient information before the event. She'd much rather go in with full knowledge of her environment, but it wasn't usually an option. "What are we looking at?"

His screen was cluttered, but he navigated the different apps and images without pause. "You were right about the building next to the bagel shop. Construction crews are remodeling, but their tile shipment was delayed, so they're not in this morning. No one else is in there." He flipped through real-estate listings and more building plans. "Nothing else with this easy kind of exit. Every other spot is too public. The tile holdup is painfully convenient."

"Stop." Something caught Kirby's attention. She reached over him, to flip back to an office-space rental. "Where is this?"

He pulled up a series of images. "It's the building next to the target's office. Two suites are empty. The rest is open twenty-four-seven, because there's a gym on the bottom floor."

It was a shitty location for a sniper. Too crowded. Bad shot angles. And she couldn't stop thinking about it.

"Ruby?" Starkad studied her.

She didn't know why he called her that, but it slipped out once, and it stuck. And it warmed her from the inside-out, to hear it. "They're wary of us by now." She was talking to herself as much as to him. "They can't jeopardize their missions with paranoia, but they'll be on alert."

"What do you want to do?"

She didn't know. Her instincts were never this split. They had to cover the obvious spot. She needed to be there. But if she was wrong, she wouldn't get to the other position in time. "We'll split up. I'll take the initial building. I need you on the secondary spot."

She hated that. They always moved together. He was her keeper, but he was also her spotter. She needed him to watch her back. She didn't trust anyone else. Not since Brit—

That was a path she wasn't tumbling down right now. She'd face that demon again tomorrow. And one last time when she looked her former partner in the eye, told her to rot in hell, and shot her.

"All right." Starkad nodded. "You ready?"

She drew in a deep breath. On the exhale, she forced out the tension, along with a brief prayer to Freya. *Help me to make peace among my enemies.* "Set."

CHAPTER TWO

Kirby was promised this new place would be amazing. Perfect for a girl like her—as in, the kind who couldn't keep a foster family for anything, because she was always in trouble for fighting.

She never started the fights, but she made sure she finished them. She hated seeing people get picked on.

The room that stretched out in front of her had cement walls and floors, and six sets of bunk beds, three on each side. It looked more like it came out of a bad movie, than like the wonderful dream life Loki promised her.

"The others are running drills," Hel said. She was tall, even for an adult. Not enough to have to duck in doorways, but she could see over the bunk beds in here without standing on tiptoe. Her white-blond hair was pulled into a tight French braid, and her T-shirt and khaki slacks hinted that the woman was as lithe and nimble as her graceful walk suggested.

"Starting tomorrow, you'll follow the same schedule as the other students in your year. Everyone begins with the basics: math, reading, one foreign language—which will become more later—physical combat, and firearms combat." As Hel spoke, she strolled down the center aisle of the room. "You're a few weeks behind, but looking at your previous test scores, I expect you'll catch up quickly. Once your specialties begin to show, your training will be adjusted."

Hel patted the bottom bunk in the rear south corner of the room. "Now that you're here, you're a member of our family. You have no family name; you'll simply be Kirby. Later in life, depending on the path you choose, that may change."

"Okay..." Kirby didn't know how she felt about that. *Family* was a bullshit word in her experience. It never meant the good things people implied it did. But her last name was *Jones*, because it was what she'd been assigned, so she wasn't attached to it.

"All of our rooms and classes are co-ed. You rise above other students based on your skill, not on what's between your legs. This bed is free. The right side of this wardrobe has clothes in your size. Take a few minutes while it's quiet, to settle in and familiarize yourself with your schedule, then join us in the cafeteria for dinner."

"Thank you." Kirby kept her fear and apprehension from her reply.

She settled onto her new bed. It was firm. No broken springs. It didn't smell like pee. Despite the dorm-like appearance, this place already had several amenities over some of the foster homes she hadn't lasted in.

She pulled her schedule from the folder Hel had given her. It was straightforward. Not much to memorize. Math. English. Latin. The three hours of physical training after classes was odd, but she'd rather have an outlet than be told to sit in her room and watch the wall.

Kirby had been in the system as long as she could remember—sometimes staying in a group home, rarely lasting with a family for more than a few months. Since no one ever told her who her mother was, she might as well have been a baby, left on the porch with a note attached to her chest.

Which should have meant she'd be adopted right away. She was blond, blue-eyed, and had been a perfectly charming baby. She knew, because she heard it every time she fucked up. *You were such a precious child. What happened?*

Now that she was a troublemaker, no one wanted her.

When a well-dressed gentleman had showed up at the group home and told her his name was Loki, she laughed in his face. Her reaction didn't seem to faze him. His deal was that she could have a new home. One where they trained people like her, to help others.

Not that she believed in superheroes, but he did spin a glorious tale. If she told him it was a stupid idea, and what he said turned out to be true, she'd never forgive herself. Maybe she'd be like Raven, from Teen Titans. Dark. Brooding. Universally powerful. Capable of summoning a dark father, to do her bidding.

It wasn't her choice to go with Loki or not, regardless. He'd shown her old place that he represented a licensed facility willing to take her, the problem child, off their hands. Now that she was a teenager, it would be even harder to place her in a foster home. She was pretty sure a large amount of money was exchanged both over and under the table.

She shuffled to her wardrobe. Jeans and T-shirts? No shit. And clean, white, cotton panties. Bras made for her pathetic boobs.

It had been so long since she had clothes this nice, that none of the old stuff fit anymore. Who cared that this was all identical? She shed everything she'd worn here and started tugging on a new outfit.

She had the underwear on and was pulling a shirt over her head, when she heard voices laughing and talking.

"Look, ladies and gents. Fresh meat."

Kirby's blood turned to ice. She didn't have to see the speaker to guess what she was about to face. This was *status quo* for her. She straightened her top, ignored that she wasn't wearing pants, and turned to face the group.

Several girls and boys about her age stood in the doorway, watching her. They spanned the rainbow in skin- and hair-color, and height. They were all thin, though, and they all wore the same jeans and T-shirt Kirby had on.

Suddenly the new clothes didn't seem so nifty.

"That's my closet, fresh meat." The guy in front sneered. He could have been the other side of Kirby's coin with his dark hair and eyes. His hard gaze made every muscle in her body tense.

Kirby's pulse hammered in her ears. Her body was on alert. She smiled, not feeling the emotion. This was fucking cliché. Someone always had to prove to the new girl how big their dick was. "It's *Kirby*. And you are?"

"Kirby? You're a pink fucking blob of stupidity?"

Charming, and then some. Kirby kind of wished she could make her eyes glow red and her voice drop two octaves, so she could say *I'm a devourer of the souls of all those who enrage me*. Too bad the words wouldn't carry the same meaning without the special effects. "That's the best you've got? Maybe try an insult a five-year-old couldn't come up with."

"How about, *get your skanky-ass backpack off my fucking bed*?" He stalked forward, until he was nose-to-nose with Kirby.

Kirby watched him walk. Noted the posture he took when he stopped. Assessed everyone else in the room and their positions. This was gonna hurt, but Kirby would be delivering a lot of the pain herself. Even if these people knew how to fight, which based on her class schedule, she assumed they would, that tended to mean their movements would be predictable. True to whatever form they'd been taught.

She was more of a *stick and move and hit back hard* kind of girl. "How about you pick on someone closer to your own IQ? Or did they bar you from the kids' dorms?"

He growled and swung. It was a tightly controlled punch, aimed straight for Kirby's head.

Kirby ducked, and the first barely clipped her cheek. She wasn't so lucky with the follow-up that landed square in her gut. She doubled over and gasped through the coughing. Her eyes watered, but she wasn't going down so easily.

He kicked.

Kirby caught his foot and twisted, yanking him to the ground.

He recovered with a sweep of his leg and drove his elbow into her cheek.

Kirby wasn't letting him draw first blood. She grabbed the short strands of his hair, pulled as hard as she could, and sank her teeth into his neck.

The bellowing shout, followed by, "You fucking bitch," was worth the mouthful of skin and the heel to the back of her knee.

A sharp whistle echoed through the room, and the flying fists stopped.

Kirby didn't have to look up to know an adult had entered the room. This was it. She'd be kicked out Day One, from this shitty place that didn't look like it was for superheroes after all, because sometimes she let delusion get the best of her, and things like that weren't real.

She wobbled to her feet, not surprised no one offered to help her.

All of the others stood at attention, like this was *Full Metal Jacket* or some shit. She wiped the back of her hand across her mouth. Only a light smear of red. Was that her blood or her opponent's? She risked a glance at the boy's neck.

Possibly a little of both.

"Mark, what happened?" Hel stood in the doorway. She wore the same impassive expression as when she'd shown Kirby to the room.

Kirby braced herself for a barrage of lies. *The new girl kicked me. She started it.*

"*Kirby* defended herself," the boy said. So he was Mark.

Kirby's retort died in her throat at his honesty, but she recovered quickly. "Damn straight, I did. No one pushes me around."

Hel extended her arm. "Come here."

Kirby wasn't going to choose now to cower. She strode across the room, back straight and eyes forward. It didn't matter she was still in just a T-shirt and panties. Or that her knee winced and her face ached and she tasted copper. She refused to show any weakness on the outside.

When Kirby drew closer, Hel grasped her hand and turned her to face the room. "These people are your teammates. You will rely on each other. Have each other's backs. They will be the reason you survive."

Then Kirby should probably try harder to hide her smugness at seeing she had broken the skin on Mark's neck with her bite. She refused to be lectured for defending herself. Which was why no one else wanted her.

"That being said"—Hel tightened her jaw—"never allow loyalty to override common sense. Betrayal will happen. Even on the inside. If they attack you again, defend yourself again. You'll fit in here just fine."

The nearly a dozen pairs of eyes glaring daggers at Kirby said otherwise.

It was going to be a long night. Mostly likely one of her staying awake, in anticipation of the next *hazing* ritual.

Over the six months that followed, the behavior that had always gotten Kirby kicked out of foster homes earned her endless praise. She struggled with that. She'd never been the best at anything before, and it was amazing, but she hated this place. Especially Mark. He was a relentless sparring partner.

She faced him on the practice mat. Her T-shirt clung to her skin from sweat, and her jeans itched. They were allowed to wear looser clothing for some of the physical education, but for hand-to-hand, they were required to stay in their street clothes. *Because,* according to Hel, *if you get in a fight on the streets, you probably won't be wearing a gi.*

Mark's feet and eyes twitched to her right.

She twisted to the left, to block, and kept moving, throwing him off balance. The asshole hadn't learned yet that if he always feinted, it was as predictable as if he never did.

He used his momentum to come up on his feet behind her. She was already facing him again. He dropped his shoulder before she could react, hit her in the stomach, and sent her stumbling.

His follow-up landed her on her back, and her hands hit the floor.

The instructor whistled to end the match. Heat flooded Kirby's face at losing again. She needed to get this. She refused to let Mark or anyone repeatedly beat her down.

Mark offered her a hand up, and she accepted, strictly for appearances. He tugged too hard, catching her off balance. It was a subtle yank—one no one would see. She stumbled into him.

"Whoa. Steady." His other hand came up to help, but not really. It was an excuse to squeeze her breast. It always was.

Kirby pushed away with a scowl and returned to her spot at the edge of the mat, so the next group could spar. She'd complained once about the overt groping. The result was being called into a room with Mark and told they needed to solve this between them. Things were the opposite of better after that.

When class was over, she broke away from the rest of the students and took a different route. Early on, she'd tested incredibly high with target shooting, so she'd been moved into sniper classes with the older students.

She didn't make any sound as she walked, so when she heard light footsteps, her stomach dropped into her shoes.

"Kirby." Mark's voice was closer than she expected.

She hadn't been paying attention. Next time—

He grabbed her arm roughly and spun her so her back was to the wall. "Where you off to so fast?" His tone was light and casual.

"Class. Same as everyone." She bit off the words.

Mark pressed the weight of his body against hers. She thought ahead several moves, trying to decide if there was any outcome where she escaped unscathed if she fought back.

He dug his fingers into her arm, applying extra pressure to a bruise he'd given her two days ago. "You've got a couple minutes for me, don't you?"

"No. I really don't." She tried to be subtle about shifting her weight, as she checked for any weaknesses in his stance.

He shoved his free hand under her shirt, yanked down her sports bra, and grabbed her breast. She bit the inside of her cheek to hide her grimace.

"Correction." He rested his lips on her ear. This close, even the soft words ached in her head. "You *always* have time for me. You're my toy, until I'm done with you."

My toy. The words snapped a taut band running through her, and her anger broke loose. She clenched her fists.

Laughter and talking echoed down the hall, accompanied by the sound of sneakers on tile.

Mark grinned and stepped back, putting several feet between them. "I won't keep you from class, Cadet."

My toy. The words looped through Kirby's thoughts through the rest of her classes. They beat in time with her fists against the punching bag, and her steps as she walked back to the dorms. They repeated in her dreams all night, and kept playing up to sparring class the next day.

She faced off against Mark on the mat and never hesitated. It was like her body took over, and her mind let it. Everything he threw at her, she blocked, side-stepped, or countered, leaving him flat on the ground when the teacher blew the whistle.

Kirby was relieved to have a hassle-free walk through the halls after, and she managed to not be alone outside of that. The next day in class, she pulled it off again. She beat Mark. *Damn*, that felt good. So did the praise that came with it. She liked being the best.

Confidence surged inside, as she strolled through the halls.

"Kirby." Mark's call sent tension through her, but her successes of the last two days shoved the feeling aside.

She whirled to face him before he could touch her, wicked smile in place. "Afternoon, Cadet."

"Do you have a minute?" His smirk probably mirrored hers.

"I don't. Not now. Not ever." History told her to cower, but she wasn't doing that, for him or anyone. "Tell you what. Walk away now, or one of two things happens."

"Oh?"

"I either hurt you in a way that lands you in the infirmary, and you can tell everyone *your toy* kicked your ass, or I can scream."

His chuckle clawed up her spine. "What good is screaming going to do you? Do you want another face-to-face, where we're told to *work things out*?"

"It's all about what I scream." She leaned in close, the way he'd done to her so many times. "If it sounds strangely like, *Holy shit, you're scared of me of all people?* then good luck convincing anyone of anything else."

His hand was pressed against her windpipe so quickly, she never saw him move. He covered her mouth. "You think you're clever." His voice was a low growl. "Everything we learn here is about more than strength and brains, and you will *never* be brutal enough to excel in this environment. But you win. You've stopped being fun. I'll find someone else, and you can remember whatever happens to them is your fault. Because I'm sure as fuck not interested in playing with a broken toy."

He let go as quickly as he'd grabbed her, and walked away without looking back.

She lingered in the hallway long after he was gone, processing the words, numbness fighting with nausea. She didn't care about the insult. What bothered her was he was right—she'd just unleashed his wrath on someone else.

CHAPTER THREE

NOW

BRIT

Brit adjusted the strap of her backpack on her shoulder, as she meandered along the downtown sidewalk. The rifle case inside dug into her shoulder blade, but it had been doing that for years. She'd be more concerned if she didn't feel the twinge of pain.

It was 7 am. If they were someplace like New York City or Tokyo, her path would be blocked by throngs of people. Here, there was breathing room. A blessing when because she and Mark were heading toward the spot where they'd set up to assassinate their target. A curse because fewer faces meant more of a chance someone would notice them.

"Why would I even do that?" she asked her partner.

This conversation hadn't changed in a few years. The details did. It was like MadLibs. Normally, she hated the fill-in-the-blank coercion that was Mark's brand of flirting. Today, she welcomed it. The grind was a reminder of why her plans were different this mission, and she didn't have the focus for a witty discussion. She needed to keep her facade in place until the last possible millisecond.

It had taken her more than three years of careful planning, to get to this spot. After half a lifetime of training with TOM, of killing on their behalf, and of putting up with this asshole's abuse, she was walking away from this life. She wouldn't fuck up her chances now. She'd have her vengeance on Mark, and whatever came after that had to be better than this hell.

"I'm not saying you would. I'm just asking you to think about it." Mark kept pace with her. She knew without looking that behind his sunglasses, his gaze swept the block every few seconds.

It was another part of their training that came as naturally as breathing, and she did the same. Searching for anything out of place. Any familiar face that might be a threat. Any obstacle that would need to be removed before they executed their mission. "I've thought. The answer's *no*. Surprised?"

He wrapped an arm around her waist and pulled her closer. Revulsion raced through her, but that was familiar as well. She rested her head on his shoulder, never breaking her surveillance. She was all too aware of the picture they painted. Her blond hair fell in a single braid down the back of her T-shirt, and her jeans were strategically faded and very designer. Mark was dressed in a similar manner. His Tee stretched tight across a defined torso, and his jeans showed he had the ass to match. To anyone else, they'd look like a twenty-something couple on their way to breakfast, or possibly trying to catch the train up to the university.

It was a mask. Everything about this life was a mask. Brit hated it. And today, she was going to rip it off and stomp it into the dirt.

"Not surprised. Just wounded." He nodded at the building up on their right. The one next to the bagel shop their target would stop at in about forty-five minutes. "Why would you pick Cabo over drinks with me Down Under?"

He was really going to make her spell it out? "Even if I didn't already have my tickets, and even if they were refundable, and even if I had any interest in visiting Australia during the winter, why would I spend my vacation with you?"

He brushed his lips over her ear, voice low. "Let's just call it *wishful thinking*."

"Not my wishes," she muttered. She'd suppressed her shiver so many times, it only nudged her gut with a hint of acid reflux. Behind her mirrored lenses, she rolled her eyes.

A trickle of doubt raced through her, as they headed toward the building. She'd told Starkad TOM would be here today. She didn't say it would be her, but that was part of her plan. The hunter who'd been taking out Brit's counterparts would be looking for this morning's team.

This wasn't the right place to be. She needed to survive long enough to beg for asylum. "Not here." She tangled her fingers with Mark's, leaned her weight into him, and nudged him across the street.

"What are you doing?" An edge crept into his voice.

Nope. She'd blocked out the torment years ago. The never accidental groping. The verbal taunts. The uninvited sex. But this was her team, and he did *not* get to determine where she shot from. "Making an executive decision and ensuring we don't become the ninth casualty."

"It's too crowded here." He walked with her, despite the protest.

They'd had weeks to study the city. Especially this block. She knew exactly how busy the gym was this time of day, and which offices on the upper floors were empty. "Then I'd better hope you're as good as you tell all the trainees."

He was. She might not trust him with her sanity, or even care for him, but like her, he was the best at what he did. And he had her back.

Only one of their classmates had been better, she'd died years ago. *Kirby.*

Brit swallowed the abrupt surge of emotion that came with the name. Today wasn't the day to let the past choke her up.

They strolled through the front door, as if they walked this route every morning, and strode past the gym without pause.

No one gave them a second glance. Most people would assume Brit and Mark worked here. Maybe they were stashing something in their offices, before coming back down to work out.

Brit didn't care what anyone assumed, as long as they forgot about her a few seconds later.

Stone pillars led to marble floors, which blended into a combination of both, lining the circular stairs. The mechanical floor counters above the two elevators in the lobby made her think the place hadn't seen a renovation in almost a hundred years. It must suck to be here in extreme temperatures, if the HVAC was the same.

A handful of people milled near the elevator, most likely having entered from an underground or back-lot parking.

She and Mark bypassed the pack of four and cut a straight line for the stairs. No one gave them more than a glance. Despite the urge to sprint to the next floor, she kept her pace even as they climbed. Seconds later, they stepped into a new hallway. To the left was a blank wall, and to the right was exactly what she anticipated—a door with a *For Lease* sign stuck to it, but no windows looking into the hallway.

Brit tuned her ears to every tiny sound that didn't belong to them. Once they were inside, it would be Mark's job to watch their surroundings and everything, while she focused on the target. Until then and after the job was complete, surveillance and awareness fell to both of them.

Except today, she'd watch her own back as she left, and he didn't realize he was her real target.

He wiggled the handle on the office door, and the *clink* of metal rattled through the corridor.

His glance and raised eyebrow said it all. *Locked.*

There was no one coming from the other end of the hallway. He leaned his shoulder into the door, and she casually turned her attention back toward the stairs.

From behind her, she heard a soft grunt, followed by a quiet *thud* as Mark strong-armed the office open. The locks were as old as everything else in this place.

They stepped into the vacant space and silently closed themselves off from the rest of the building. The time for public performance and idle chatter was over. From this point on, their only communication would be what was necessary to get the job done.

A maze of filing cabinets led to a stack of waiting-room chairs, lining the far wall. Other than that and the dust floating through the air in the morning sun, the room was empty.

Without exchanging words, she dropped to one knee and pulled off her backpack, while he made his way to the window. He fiddled with three latches until one gave way without protest and cracked open six inches on the bottom. Another thing to love about the older buildings. The new high rises didn't have any opening widows.

She extracted a black polymer case from her bag, lay it on the ground, and opened it. She pulled several metal and plastic components from inside.

Mark peered out the window at something on the street below. "Clean shot. Less than a hundred meters."

She snarled at his back, and let the irritation slide into her voice. "I need a more accurate range, and check the GPS for wind speed and direction."

"Ninety meters. A hundred meters. What's the difference?"

He did this every fucking time. Compared to most of his bullshit, it was tame. Except that here, their lives were on the line. "Those ten meters are the difference between a clear head shot and only getting your ear blown off."

Today, ten inches would get his head blown off. She kept the thought from her expression.

"Fine. Ninety-four point nine." He stepped back from the window.

She arranged the parts in front of her in the same pattern that repetitive training had drilled into her, and then set about assembling the AUG-HBAR-T sniper rifle.

She took her spot at the open window. Sliding behind her weapon, she opened the bolt. She stopped for a moment to bow her head. *Vidar guide my hand and escort my enemies to Hel.*

She reached for the high-capacity magazine. Leaning the weapon forward and up, careful not to disturb the bipod's footing, she slid the ammunition into its receiver. She angled the rifle down with practiced precision and put her shoulder into it, trying to ignore the ambivalence the action always filled her with. Reaching forward, she removed the caps covering both ends of the scope, then peered through. The fire zone was clear and unobstructed.

Even better, with the foot traffic light, she should be able to spot the target, accomplish her goals, and beat a hasty retreat before anyone realized the shot came from here.

She rested her finger on the trigger, closed her eyes, and exhaled. *Is this all I am?* The question echoed in her mind, as it did during every mission. She shook the thought away. "Status?"

"Time is O-seven-thirty-five. Range is ninety-five point one meters. GPS check as of O-seven-twenty-two reported the temperature at thirteen degrees, steady winds from the North-Northwest at three point two kilometers per hour, and clear skies with thirty-two percent relative humidity."

She twisted two of the knobs on the scope, one click each, and turned her head toward him, memorizing where he sat.

She raised an eyebrow as he hooked a pair of fragmentation grenades into the waistband of his jeans. That was unusual for him. Did he know what she was up to? No. He was taking precautions, the same way she had by choosing this spot.

"Overkill, much?" she asked.

He tapped the plastic handle of the MP-5 lying on the table next to his open bag, eyes never leaving his range-finder. "It never hurts to be prepared".

"For what? The Huns?"

"You have your job, I have mine. Fire zone is clear. Our guest should arrive in approximately— On the clock, shooter." His tone changed mid-sentence. "Target spotted, one hundred twenty-four meters, east side of street, heading north at a casual pace. Target is alone."

Her cheer vanished. She turned her head and buried her right eye in the scope. A familiar head of strawberry-blond hair—identical to the photos—filled her sight. "Target confirmed. Safety off. Tracking target."

The target continued on its route, occasionally obscured by the heads of the other people on the street. The tension of the moment stretched the perception of time in the abandoned office. After a brief eternity, the target stumbled and dropped her purse.

"I have a shot. Engaging target." She spoke the words, but didn't apply pressure to the trigger. She had a blink to get this right. To announce she was firing. Ensure Mark was focused on the street below. Pull the pistol from the holster at her waist and shoot him.

"Wait. Target has a little friend."

The unexpected statement startled her, but she maintained her focus. "Where?"

"In our old spot. *Fuck.* Change target priority," Mark ordered. "Second floor. Missing window pane, three windows in, one pane down."

Brit ignored his command. He was distracted, and she just needed to say her lines. "Engaging target one."

She reached for her pistol. Something collided with her shoulder, and pain jolted through her body. The impact threw her back. She tried to reach for either weapon, but her fingers didn't work right. Why did it hurt so much? "*Status.*"

"*Grenade,*" Mark shouted as he hooked an arm around her waist and half-dragged her behind the filing cabinets.

They crashed hard onto the floor, Mark's 100 kilos knocking the wind out of her. A blinding flash filled the room, as a concussion wave drove them into the far wall. Another burst of pain erupted through her shoulder.

Her world turned cold and gray, and sparkles danced across her field of vision. Mark's movements seemed slow and deliberate. The sounds that reached her ears were distant. Filtered. She felt weightless.

I must be diving. Mark floated above her, an unusual look of fear and concern on his face.

Is he actually worried about me? The question surfaced from nowhere and made her gut churn. It didn't help her make sense of the patterns his lips formed, though. She focused with what intellectual resources were available to her.

Oh. I know that word. A chill ran the length of her spine and a drop of reason trickled into her thoughts. A single word passed through her mind and made her blood run cold, before pain stole her consciousness. *Kirby.*

Chapter Four

10 Years Ago
Kirby

Kirby lay on her top bunk, listening to the breathing of the other students in the room. She waited until it was all either steady breathing or low snores.

Tension cranked through her. No one knew she did this. If they found out, the past two years here would be nothing, compared to the torment and ridicule she would receive.

She didn't have it as bad as some of the students. The unspoken rule was *only the strong survive.* So Kirby had ensured that she wasn't just strong; she was the strongest.

That made her a different kind of target. And it was exhausting—always sleeping with one eye open, being the cadet everyone wanted to best or silence…

On nights when it got to be too much, when the pressure and torment and backhanded comments swelled to the point where her head and heart threatened to burst from the anguish, she waited until everyone was asleep, then snuck into the bathrooms and sought solitude.

She hopped from her bed, hitting the ground without making a sound. Her footsteps were silent, as she crossed the room and slipped into the hallway.

She paused, ears strained for any out-of-place sound. She knew what it sounded like when the foundation settled and the HVAC kicked on, and the weather was anything more than calm outside.

Tonight, all was clear. She padded through the corridor. The community-style showers were too open for her to have any privacy, but there were stalls in the restrooms. She could lock the door to one on the end, pull her feet up so no one could see her, and enjoy the silence.

As Kirby stepped into the room, she heard a faint sob echo off the tile. The noise vanished. She listened. Someone was breathing and trying to be quiet.

There were no feet visible under the stalls, and some of the doors looked shut, but she wouldn't be able to tell if any were locked without trying them.

She stepped closer to the sinks, staying at a distance that would keep whoever was in here from seeing the shadows or her feet, and followed the noises to the far end of the room.

Another tiny sob escaped from the other side of the metal door. Kirby knew the kind of hurt and frustration that caused that. It shook her to her core. "Hello?" she said softly.

All the sound stopped. Even the breathing.

She nudged open the adjacent door, hopped on the toilet, and looked down at a girl trying to make herself look very small. Brit was a year younger than Kirby, and fairly talented.

"Hey." Kirby kept her voice quiet. She shoved her frustration aside and focused instead on the way her heart broke for the other girl.

Brit looked up, brown eyes wide and red rimmed. Her jaw dropped open, and she backed up against the wall. "Please, don't tell anyone. You can hit me if you want. Just don't let anyone know I was crying."

"I won't tell anyone, and I won't hit you. I don't do that to anyone who doesn't deserve it." Kirby could pounce on the situation. Teach Brit how wrong it was to let her vulnerability show. But an empty ache throbbed in Kirby's chest. Maybe she wasn't the only one who needed a friend.

Brit unfolded a little. "I deserve it."

"Why would you say that?"

"Because I'm weak."

Kirby pulled herself the rest of the way up, hopped the dividing wall, and landed on her feet in front of Brit. "You'll get stronger. That's the point of training."

"It's hard." Brit wiped her hand across her face. "I'm trying, but my student teacher says I'll never get better. And he's right. Every time I think I've got it, he points out where else I've failed."

A sour taste rose in the back of Kirby's throat, mingling with her sympathy for Brit. She knew that description all too well. Mark's words mocked her. *I'll find another toy. One who's fun. That's on you.*

"Who is it?" she asked.

"I'm not saying." Brit's eyes were huge again, and her terror-filled voice grew in volume. "It's on me. I'm the one who needs to get better."

Kirby placed a finger against her lips. "*Shh.* Is it Mark?"

"Why would you ask that? Everyone loves Mark. He's one of the best. He teaches us to grow beyond our boundaries."

That confirmed it.

Kirby crouched, to bring herself to eye level with Brit. "He's an asshole and a bully." She spoke so softly, she barely heard her own voice. "He gets off on hurting you. I guarantee it."

"I just need to get better."

Kirby rested a hand on Brit's knee. "You do, yes. We all do. The way he teaches isn't going to give you that. I'll take care of this for you." It wasn't a question of *maybe*. She had to fix this. It was her fault Mark was focused on someone else, and she could bring that attention back to herself. She was far enough along in her training she could handle it.

"If you go after him, he'll know it's my fault. He'll—"

"Make your life miserable?" Kirby raised an eyebrow. "He already does. Listen, we're supposed to trust each other unless we see a reason to do otherwise, right?"

Brit shrugged.

"I swear on my rankings that I can handle him, and he won't know you were involved."

"How?"

Kirby frowned, and the gnawing pit of dread grew inside. *By taking the focus off you and putting it back on me.* "If I tell you, it'll be harder to say you didn't know."

"Why would you help a nobody like me? That doesn't get you anywhere."

Kirby studied Brit while she searched for an answer. She'd help regardless. This place seemed determined to suck the soul from the students and replace it with ice and steel. Kirby didn't want to go through that, and no one else should have to either. This conversation made her think that wouldn't cut it as an answer. "Everyone knows who you are. The older kids, all of us—you're the best there is with a scope."

Pink spread across Brit's cheeks. "I'm not bad."

"Always own your accomplishments." Kirby squeezed Brit's leg and stood. "You earned that distinction. Be proud of it." She reached behind her and unlocked the stall door. "And don't worry about Mark. I'm sure he'll come around."

Brit gave her a half-smile. That was kind of cute. "Okay. I trust you. And thank you."

KIRBY

Kirby stood at the back of the classroom, watching the younger students—Brit's class—prep to spar. Mark stepped to the front of the room. He'd earned *student teacher* status a few months back. If Kirby had known what he'd do with it…

What? She would have said something to someone? That hadn't worked in the past. So today, she had a different solution. She'd pulled a lot of strings to get permission to put on a demonstration with him. And she'd promised to let him know beforehand.

She'd lied about that bit.

"Cadet," she called as she strode up to him. Anxiety churned inside. She'd just passed the point of no return. Doing this meant she took his wrath back. She knew how to handle it, though, even better than two years ago. She wouldn't let anyone else put up with his bullshit. "Are you interested in showing your class how this is actually done?"

His cold smile gnawed at the lining of her gut. He gave a deep bow, his gaze never leaving her. "The pleasure would be mine."

Kirby moved into an at-ease stance, feet shoulder-width apart, hands clasped behind her back. "How do you want to start?"

"I'll allow you to choose." Sarcasm lined Mark's deference. "What do you prefer?"

She was so much better than last time they'd fought. Then again, so was he. Her specialty was still sniping, while his was more physical. It didn't matter. She knew how to play the psychological games, and his ego was his weakness. "Attack me," she said.

He lunged, and she sidestepped, left foot extending to catch his right, turning with him as he fell, and planting a knee in the small of his back.

The lightest whisper of laughter rippled through the room.

Kirby extended a hand to her fallen sparring partner, the way he had done to her so many times.

He slapped away her offer of help and stood.

She fell back into a loose posture. "I'm sorry. You weren't ready. Try again?"

Mark brushed a loose strand of hair out of his brown eyes, took a deep breath, and lunged again. Kirby stepped aside again, arm flying straight out to her side, striking him in the diaphragm. He halted with an *oof*, and she kicked out her foot, catching him in the back of the knee and dropping him to all fours. Panting, he struggled to catch his breath.

She stepped around him, to face the class. "Who here understands the purpose of this demonstration?"

Several pairs of eyes grew wide. Probably because she'd turned her back on a pissed-off opponent. Mark got noisy and reckless when he was angry. She heard him climb to his feet and lunge.

She dropped to one knee, landing her shoulder in his gut. One hand flew to his collar, and the other to his crotch. Using his momentum to carry him forward, she flipped him to land on his back and audibly knocked the wind out of him. He whimpered when she twisted his balls enough to be threatening, before letting go.

Kirby would pay for that, but *fuck*, it felt good right now. She stood, not even winded. "While I appreciate Cadet Mark's helping to demonstrate that an opponent doesn't always fight fair, that's not what we're here to learn." She nodded at a boy in the back of the room. "Help your student teacher to the infirmary." She swallowed her pleased giggle.

Her amusement shriveled when Mark met her gaze, his eyes narrowed and his jaw clenched. She kept her mask in place, despite her inner turmoil.

"Lesson learned," he growled in a voice meant only for her ears, before he brushed off the offer of help and strode from the room.

And there it was. Until he graduated, her life would be hell.

Chapter Five

Kirby

Kirby was in her spot near the under-reconstruction building. Watching. Waiting.

Something wasn't right.

She itched to go find Starkad. The TOMs should have arrived already. Instinct told her to leave. Training insisted she cover her bases, because walking away left a possible attack vector exposed.

And then Starkad hissed into her ear piece, "You're in the wrong spot. Move. Now."

She was sprinting before he finished. "On my way."

"It's too late. Target's walking out of the bagel shop." Starkad's tone was hard, hammering in her ear as she ran.

There was only one position in the other building where they could be. Kirby spotted the open window in a glance. If she ran down to the street, everyone would see her draw her weapon.

The panic would make things worse. Her arrest wouldn't help either.

She ran to the second floor of the empty building, forcing herself not to count the seconds ticking away. When she reached a room with a good view of the spot across the street, she chambered a stun grenade in her GL06 and shattered the nearest window.

Freya, guide my hand and sight.

She aimed the weapon on an arc, fired, and was retreating before the projectile landed.

It would hit her target. It would be contained to their room. No one else would be hurt, but whoever the TOMs of the day were, they'd be off-balance, giving her time to get to them.

The explosion reached her ears when she was halfway down the stairs. By the time she hit the street, chaos had erupted.

She should have thought of this. She had to be careful with the way she forced her way through the crowds, to keep from drawing attention to herself.

At least ditching the bags was an option. A team would recover them later, but if law enforcement got to them first, they couldn't be traced back to Kirby or the people she worked for.

Starkad would already be there. She needed to find that balance between beating a fast path to her destination and not drawing attention.

"Watch it, man. I didn't do anything." Starkad's voice sounded in her ear. He wasn't talking to her, though. "Whoa. Do I look like the kind of guy to carry a grenade, officer?"

Well, *fuck*. She was on her own. She itched to go check on him, but training wouldn't let her. He'd be fine, and she needed to finish the job.

The flash of time it took for her to cross the street seemed like an eternity. She hit the back of the building, to avoid the evacuated crowds, and sprinted up a set of service stairs.

She reached the room the TOMs had been in. Frustration built inside at the lack of bodies—living or otherwise. She never let a target get away.

The backpack by the window wouldn't tell her anything. It was as impossible to trace as the gear she'd dumped. But the AUG next to it…

Kirby needed to turn around now and leave. Find Starkad and regroup. The gun knocked loose a trickle of memories she didn't want. Every one of her former classmates had their weapon of choice. Most stuck with the standard issue M40A5.

Kirby crossed the room, despite the voice screaming in her head to leave now. This was one of the most idiotic things she'd ever done, and that was saying a lot. She had to know. She toed the rifle, and the hash marks on the stock glared in the morning light. *Brit.*

Her heart dropped into her stomach, which plummeted into her shoes. She'd known this day would come. Why did it have to be now?

"*Hands in the air,*" shouted a sharp voice behind her.

BRIT

Brit was in about fifty shades of pain. She knew how to shake it off, but not so much at once. She had no idea how she made the short walk to their car. Each footstep jarred through her shoulder.

She'd dislocated it, for sure. The thought didn't ease the agony, but it forced her to compartmentalize and assess.

Mark opened the back door for her, and she collapsed on the rear seat with an *oof*.

"I've got this," he said and pulled a blanket over her. Not to hide her, but on the off chance police were stopping cars, she'd be the girlfriend who got sick on their vacation.

Blackness licked the edges of her vision as he drove. The car was moving at a crawl, and she was pretty sure that wasn't only because her head was swimming.

Mark hit a dip in the road, and the car bounced, jarring her shoulder. A new spike of pain seared through her body and stole her consciousness.

Brit's eyes flew open, her heart hammering against her ribcage, and heat screaming through her arm. Her pulse slowed as her surroundings solidified around her. The hotel was visible through the car's rear window. Her shoulder throbbed each time she moved or thought, but her arm wouldn't budge.

The car door opened, and Mark's face appeared over hers. He cocked an eyebrow. "Thank *Forseti* you're awake." His concern was bullshit. He just hated the idea that someone besides him got to hurt her. "The last thing I need is to explain to hotel staff why I'm carrying an unconscious woman into my room."

"Glad I didn't inconvenience you." Brit's voice cracked in her dry throat, softening her sarcasm.

Walking didn't hurt any more than lying down, but she had to lean into Mark, to keep from stumbling like she was drunk. In their hotel room, she stepped into the bathroom. Blood and sweat matted her hair to her head. Her arm hung limply at her side, and the skin peeking out from under her sleeve was swollen and turning purple.

Dislocated shoulder and ruptured eardrum. The former was going to suck to set. The latter meant she wasn't flying for the next month. Lovely.

That meant they could stay here.

Why did she want that? Her brain twitched when she burrowed through her memories for snippets of activity before unconsciousness. She'd had the target in her sight. Everything was going the way it should have, and then… A black spot sat in her brain where the rest should be.

Stupid unconsciousness. Her head pounded in protest, as she pushed for memories that might have been lost when she'd been knocked out. How had she been knocked out? Her shoulder pulsed with the agony of something she couldn't quite grasp.

Kirby. The two syllables echoed in Brit's skull. *Fuck.* Her world swam, blurring at the corners of her vision, and her gut churned. She swallowed back the mud of emotion churning inside and straightened. That couldn't be right. Kirby was dead. Because of Brit.

But apparently Starkad had lied about that—go figure—and Kirby was hunting her own.

Correction. They weren't hers anymore. Because of Brit.

Brit grabbed a glass from the counter, filled it with lukewarm water, and chugged it in a single swallow.

Her stomach protested. She heaved several times, before bringing her breathing under control. Her throat wasn't so parched now. That was a step in the right direction.

"On the toilet seat. Sit." Mark's command dragged her from the unpleasant tumble into the past.

She didn't have the strength to argue. Maybe she'd heard him wrong. She didn't see Kirby. Her mind had been playing tricks on her earlier. "What did you say? In the building?"

"You know what I said." He ran the faucet, testing the temperature every few seconds, then grabbed a washcloth.

She pointed at her damaged ear. "I couldn't hear."

"A ghost is hunting us." He clenched his fist. "They didn't want her in Valhalla, and Freya wouldn't take her, so Kirby is back to fucking haunt us. I watched her fire a fucking grenade at us, and she didn't even have the respect to frag our asses. A flash bomb. That's what we got."

Because Kirby hadn't wanted collateral damage. Brit wasn't going to argue that detail. She hadn't just brought wrath down on them, by telling Starkad where to find their people. She'd summoned the Mistress of Hel.

"We have to take her out." Brit didn't want anything to do with Kirby. Not to hunt her. Not to save her. Not to ever seeing her fucking face again, despite what the raging conflict inside said. But this was Brit's excuse to stay here. To get a chance to beg Starkad and the people he worked with for asylum.

"We have to hop in a car and drive our asses out of this truck stop of a town, like protocol dictates." Mark knelt in front of her and pressed the washcloth to her face.

She hissed at the heat, then sank into his gentle ministrations as he wiped her face and the side of her head clean.

"Please?" She made herself sound submissive and swallowed the surge of bile that came with even pretending to bow to Mark. "Let me do this. Let *us* do this."

He clenched his jaw, and his nostrils flared. "I'll tell command we haven't confirmed the status of the target. You have to do something for me, though." He lightly grasped the hand on her bad arm and looked her in the eye. He trailed his fingers up to settle on her shoulder, so lightly she barely felt his touch.

"Favor for a favor is fair."

"Suck my cock."

She wasn't in the mood for this. Rage spilled inside. "You fucking assh— *FUUUUUUUUUCK*." Her anger bled into a piercing scream when he twisted her shoulder back into the socket. The pain clawed at her senses, threatening unconsciousness.

He caught her as she wobbled and started to fall. He scooped her up and carried her to the bed.

She was too drained and hurt too much to summon a reply. *Stupid fucking sadistic asshole.* "I hate you."

His smile swam in and out of her vision, as she struggled to keep from passing out. "I know." He vanished from her field of vision.

She heard a zipper and him rummaging through luggage, then the water running again.

He returned. "Pain pills."

"Percocet?"

"Ibuprofen. I'll ask Command if they can get you anything stronger when I tell them our stay's been extended." He handed over the drugs, then the water.

Because the one time he wasn't carrying something that would knock her out was the one time she wanted it. She swallowed both and sank back onto the mattress. Her shoulder was on fire, and her stomach was threatening to pack its bags and leave via her throat. But she was focused on two words. *Kirby* and *freedom.*

Would she have to reconcile with one, to achieve the other? She didn't know if she could do that. She didn't know if it was even an option, from Kirby's perspective.

Chapter Six

8 Years Ago
Kirby

Kirby practically skipped to her next class. At seventeen, she was specializing. She wasn't just good, she was the best, and she was about to become the youngest student yet to move on to the real world. Though Brit was catching her quickly. In fact, Brit was joining the advanced martial arts this afternoon.

Excitement bubbled inside Kirby every time she thought about it. They'd have a class together. That meant more time together, even if it was just being in the same room. Brit was the one and only friend Kirby had. On a lot of days, friendship wasn't enough, but Kirby was terrified if she said *I like you. A lot*, that it would destroy what they had.

She was content to hang out, have fun, and now train together.

Mark headed toward her with a small crowd. He'd made a hobby of tormenting her, but these days it was *status quo*. She could block out the cruelty, the unwanted sex, and the bruises, since him focusing on her meant he wasn't doing it to someone else.

Still, it took effort to put on the mask she wore around him, and she wasn't in the mood to be fake this close to her favorite class.

He passed her with a curt nod, and some of her tension drained away. She wouldn't relax completely until she was in the classroom, though.

A hard body pressed into her back, and an arm wrapped around her waist. He caught her off guard and easily pulled her into a side hallway. She could struggle, but she didn't.

"You've been avoiding me." He molded his body to hers.

Revulsion slid over her. This was the game. She'd live through worse once she got in the field. He was practice. She just had to remember that. "No, I haven't. I have class twenty-four-seven, like everyone in this place."

"Mhm." His erection was obvious through his jeans, as he pressed into her. "I hear you're being assigned to a team soon." He glided his hand down to her ass and squeezed.

"It's true. I am." She could hurt him in so many ways right now. He was distracted. Exposed. An elbow to the windpipe or gut, a knee to the balls, and he'd be left gasping. Or she could break his wrist with a simple twist of their bodies.

She let him roam his hands over her instead. His attentions were a minor inconvenience. As long as he focused on her, he wasn't looking at someone else. The series of excuses for letting him have his way came so easily these days, she barely registered their meaning.

"I've put in a request for us to be teamed up," he said. "You're brilliant with a rifle, and I love watching your back. We'd make an amazing team."

Except they wouldn't. She didn't trust him. She wouldn't cross the room to spit on him if he was on fire. "We just might."

"That also means time on the road together. Shared rooms." He dipped his head and bit her neck hard enough to leave a mark. "We can do everything I've ever wanted."

"I'm looking forward to it." The words burned up her throat. "But I'm not going to be assigned to anyone if you make me late for class." Her sugary tone never faltered.

He stepped back. "Oh, love. We both know no one is going to demote or hold you back. You're TOM's shining star. But I wouldn't want to mar your perfect record."

"Thanks." She stepped around him and did her best job of hurrying to class without looking like she was in a rush. Her good mood was gone, lost in the horrific possibility of life with Mark after school. It was supposed to be over after he moved on. No more torment. Freedom for her. If they were teamed up...

"*Cadet*." Starkad's sharp call cut through her spiraling thoughts. "Are you joining us?"

"Yes, sir. Sorry, sir." She took her spot in the front row of the classroom.

He was their combat instructor. Everyone hated him as a teacher. He was demanding. Abrupt.

Offered no leeway. But no one ever complained about being in his class—especially not the girls. He was the best the school had for hand-to-hand combat. And he was sexy as fuck. Blond. Built. Tattooed. Basically a modern-day Viking.

It was a shame he wasn't the Seduction instructor. Kirby would climb him in a heartbeat. When thoughts of being with Brit didn't tease her fantasies at night, she was dreaming of Starkad taking her. Sure, daydreaming about a teacher was dangerous, but it wasn't as though she was going to act on it. Not the way some of the students had tried to do.

Still, the things he could probably teach her...

She squeezed her legs together, to suppress the insistent throb.

"Now that we're all here..." He strolled along the front of the class, casting random glances at the students. "Cadet Brit is joining us today. Everyone treat her the way you would anyone else."

Which, in his classroom, was with respect. Another thing Kirby adored about him.

"Let's pair off. You and you. You and you." Starkad pointed as he spoke, pairing everyone up. "You and you."

Kirby's heart sank when he pointed to her and Brit. She never sparred with the younger girl. In practice or anywhere. It wasn't because Brit was bad. She wouldn't be in this class if she wasn't one of the best. But Kirby couldn't make herself go all-out with Brit, who deserved better. Brit needed someone who wouldn't hold back.

"Assign me someone else," Kirby said.

Starkad narrowed his gaze. "Everyone else already has a partner."

"A partner you assigned. Give me someone else."

Whispers fluttered through the room like butterflies. Starkad snapped his fingers. "Cadet Kirby, my office. Now." He pointed at the door behind him.

She had a lot of fantasies that included those words, but none of them evoked the terror his current expression did.

He looked at the rest of the class. "No one talks while I'm gone. You talk, you sit this round out, and it goes on your record as refusing to participate."

That was enough of a threat to keep the students in line. Like Kirby, they were all months from being assigned to a team and field work. To becoming what they'd trained for. To heading out into the world, unsupervised.

Kirby marched toward his office with her back straight. The instant she was inside, he slammed the door shut behind her.

"What the fuck are you doing?" His quiet question was far more threatening than if he'd yelled.

"I can't fight her. I'm not capable." Kirby didn't know why she told him the truth. She should have come up with an excuse, but the reality slipped out before she could give it a second thought. Worse, her body was reacting to him being this close. Anticipation raced over her skin. Her mind treated her to vivid images of him, pushing her onto the desk and ripping off her top. Of him sliding inside her.

That was so not what she needed to be thinking about.

"You'll fight her." His words were clipped.

Kirby shook her head. "I won't. I'll take whatever punishment you administer instead." *Spank me, please*. That needed to stop.

He clenched his jaw, and for a few seconds, the only sound in the room were the grunts of the other students, fighting. "You're not just setting yourself up, by doing this," he finally said. "You've set a bad precedent for her. Now she's the girl who's not good enough for my star pupil to spar with."

No. That was the last thing Kirby wanted. "So when she fights someone else, she'll prove that's not true, and it will be far more effective evidence than if she fights me."

"You'll face off with Brit, and you won't pull your punches."

"Nope." Kirby shook her head. This was a stupid hill to die on, but she couldn't do what he asked. She couldn't bring herself to hit Brit.

"I see." Starkad stepped around her and rested his hand on the doorknob. "You've made your stance clear. Back to class."

She hadn't won that easily. What was he setting her up for?

They rejoined the rest of the class, and he clapped. "At ease, cadets."

Everyone fell back into their rows. Kirby joined them as the only student besides Brit who wasn't flushed and sweating. Brit wouldn't meet her gaze.

Starkad was right. How did Kirby not consider the consequences of her actions sooner?

Starkad stood in front of them. "Cadet Kirby is intimidated by the fresh meat."

Despite the hush in the room, she swore she heard the mental snickers. That was fine. She'd been picked on for five years, and she was good enough to prove herself.

"So Brit will join a different group, and the three of them will trade off."

What was going on? Kirby clenched her fists until her nails dug into her palms.

"And Cadet Kirby will spar with me," Starkad said.

Well, *fuck*. Kirby kept her surprise and concern from her face, and stepped forward. She was the best in her class. She could hold her own against the teacher for at least a couple of seconds.

This was to help Brit save face and keep Kirby from fighting her. It was worth it.

Starkad took his spot across from her on the mat. She held his gaze, alert for any hint or sign of what came next. He was behind her before she saw him twitch, pinning her arm to her back with enough force to make her grunt in pain. Half a tug more, and he'd break something.

She bit the inside of her cheek, to keep from whimpering.

He let go. "You weren't ready. Let's try again."

White-hot embarrassment flooded her face. She'd watched him teach for more than a year. She could guess how he'd open next, if she focused.

He executed a move she'd never seen before, that had her twisted on her back, his weight on her thigh this time. If he brought his knee down, he'd break her femur.

He let her up.

Nothing about his movements was choreographed. He didn't give anything away in his eyes or the twitch of his muscles. There was no time for her to react.

By now, she had to be red from the embarrassment. This was worse than what she'd done to Mark all those years ago. She looked like she was standing still, letting him hit her.

"One more time," he said. "Pay attention, Ruby."

What did he call her? Was that because her face was so dark? *Freya*, how humiliating. But she watched. She turned all of her skill and training inward, and grasped something she didn't know was there. A hint about what he'd do next.

Kirby couldn't say how she saw it coming, but she recognized his attack the instant his foot flew toward her flank. Her muscles reacted without her input. She countered. She twisted. She stepped inside his reach threw him off-balance.

Unlike a student sparring partner, he recovered in an instant. He sprang back to his feet and used her momentum against her. He brought his foot down on her ankle.

Her scream slipped out before she could cut it off, and she crumpled to the ground in pain.

Starkad snapped. "You." He pointed at a boy in the back. "Take her to the infirmary. Her ankle is broken, so make sure she doesn't put any weight on it."

Kirby limped away, shame and pain raging inside.

The doctor told her she'd sustained a spiral fracture, but it was clean. If she kept her weight off it until it was healed and followed her physical therapy strictly, she'd be walking again in six to eight weeks, and fully recovered in three months.

Kirby kept her grumbling to herself, about all the physical activity she'd need to catch up on after being off her feet for so long. She couldn't ignore the whisper of relief that pointed out, this way, she wouldn't be assigned to work with Mark.

She still had to do her academic work, and there was upper-body and sniper practice she could participate in. It kept her from going stir crazy, but she hated being stuffed back in the infirmary, night after night. It was easier to keep her there than maneuver her in and out of the dorms.

After two weeks, Kirby hadn't seen Brit at all. How badly had she fucked up? She'd been worried about destroying their friendship by confessing her love, and now she'd ruined things anyway. She'd have to grovel as soon as she was capable.

When Starkad stepped into the room one night, she was surprised. He sent the nurse away and pulled a chair up next to Kirby's bed.

The harsh lines on his face that seemed etched in place during class were gone. He straddled the chair and rested his arms on the back. "I'm sorry

I had to do that." He nodded at her foot. There was nothing but sincerity in his voice.

"You did what you needed to, and so did I." She wasn't sure what to make of the situation. He was even sexier outside of the classroom. Casual. Almost sad. And his eyes were a piercing blue.

"You can't do this. Never again," he said softly. "You can never show favoritism in here. I don't care how much you love or adore that girl, you hide those feelings like they're the most precious secret in the universe." He almost sounded like he spoke from experience.

A pleasant shiver raced up Kirby's spine. Who had he loved? Was it another instructor? A student?

She wanted to deny how she felt about Brit, but the words wouldn't come. "Why?"

"You know you have enemies in here, don't you?"

All too well. She kept her mouth shut and shoved Mark's image from her mind.

"They'll use your affection against you. They'll use it to destroy you. That's why the school has a no-fraternization policy, and we aren't teaching you to be best friends with each other. Not because we care if cadets fuck each other. It's because you've all been trained to spot anyone's weakness and use it to your advantage."

Right. Trust everyone, unless they give you a reason not to. Then stab them in the back. Beautiful contradiction. "I understand."

Starkad worked his jaw. The way his gaze lingered on her made her heart skip a beat. She was just a silly girl with a silly crush, like half of the students in here, and there was no way he was watching her with affection.

He stood with a heavy sigh. "I'll see you back in class in a few months."

"All right." Her smile was genuine. She couldn't help but watch him walk from the room. Lusting after him was at least as dangerous as wanting to be with Brit, but he was just a fantasy.

Nothing more.

Chapter Seven

NOW

GWYDION

Gwydion tried to stay away. He'd never liked Starkad's decision to hide and isolate Kirby, but he'd complied because the berserker was right. They needed to try something new, to keep Kirby from dying.

But she hadn't been a TOM for a couple of years. She'd been on the outside, with Starkad keeping her all to himself. And Gwydion was sick of waiting. He had to see Kirby.

He'd called in a favor with a friend in Urd, to find out where she'd be next. The kind of thing that would cost him a minor miracle in the future. Kirby was worth it. Fortunately, that friend was Min, who relented because Gwydion wasn't the only one tired of waiting to talk to Kirby.

He was strolling down Main Street in Salt Lake City, when an explosion burst through the windows above a twenty-four hour gym. The noise and flash summoned images of the past. Screams erupted around him, and the crowds pressed in. War after war overlapped in his mind. Terror bled into death, and then into battlefields piled with bodies. Sand that didn't exist clogged his lungs. The whistle of the train became falling mortars in his head.

He could push past this. He tapped his index and middle finger in an alternating rhythm against his leg, and focused on the pattern. It figured—immortality granted him physical immunity from almost everything he encountered, but it didn't cure the trauma of having fought in several major wars and a handful no one had heard of, over the last fifteen hundred years.

Focusing on the drum of his fingers helped center him. A movement caught his attention and he turned. *Kirby*. She was a few feet away, weaving through the crowd and heading for the explosion.

It didn't matter that she was dressed in baggy, filthy clothes, that her hair was currently auburn instead of blond, or that she wore a fierce scowl. Her face was seared in his dreams, and seeing her sent sparks racing along his skin.

This was the wrong time to approach her. He wouldn't put her life in danger by distracting her. She entered the building through the back. She'd see if he followed.

When a group of police approached, concern ratcheted inside.

It was a matter of suggestion, to make himself look like one of them. He was a trickster god with a gift for impersonation. Adopting the illusion of the same uniforms they wore and fogging their minds to make them believe he'd always been with them was as simple as flipping a switch.

If only it were as simple to send Kirby a mental warning to get the fuck out now.

He stuck with the officers as they searched the first floor. Most everyone had evacuated. No Kirby. Maybe she was clear.

On the second floor, the layout wasn't as open. All of the doors were closed but one. Gwydion's stress cranked to *full blast*. The officers approached with guns drawn.

The man in front toed the door open.

Kirby stood near the window, staring at a rifle that lay at her feet.

What are you doing? Gwydion screamed in his head. *Why are you still here?*

"Hands in the air," one of the officers shouted.

She complied instantly.

"Hands on the back of your head, and walk backward toward us."

Influencing them to think he was one of them, that he should be there, was one thing. They were distracted and didn't care, as long as he wasn't a threat. Could he twist a group of high-strung thoughts to not have itchy trigger fingers?

Kirby did as ordered. When she was within arm's reach, one officer holstered his gun, jerked her arms down, and cuffed her, before spinning her to face them.

Her expression was one of terror. Unshed tears glistened in her wide eyes. She studied her shoes. "I didn't touch anything. I swear. I wanted to see what happened, and maybe that gun is worth some money, you know? It's got to be. It's one of those expensive machine guns, right?"

"What are you doing up here?" Someone demanded.

She shrank back. "Everyone was running away. I wanted to see if there was anything up here I could sell. Can I have a buck?"

If she was even half of what Starkad said, this was an act. She knew what was on the floor, and she could John Wick these uniforms without breaking a sweat.

But she had Gwydion convinced. He wanted to wrap her up. Save her. Take her away from this cruel world and give her whatever she asked for. Then again, he'd want to do that anyway. The homeless-and-hungry act simply amplified existing urges.

The officer who had cuffed her pulled her closer. "Do you have any weapons on you? Anything sharp? Razors. Needles?" As he spoke he ran rough hands over her arms. Inside her jacket sleeves. When he grabbed her chest, she whimpered and tried to pull away.

The officer smirked. He shoved his hand in every pocket. Spent several seconds groping her inner thighs and crotch, as she squirmed and folded in on herself.

Gwydion's blood boiled. If he killed them all now, just sent the thought through each of their heads that caused blood vessels to burst, their lives would end a few decades early, but in a century, it wouldn't matter.

It would also turn this mess into a manhunt for a cop killer. While a flash grenade would spark an investigation, as long as no one died, the same passion and lack of reason wouldn't drive their actions.

"She's just some homeless kid." Gwydion forced his tone to sound dismissive. "Look at the bitch. Bad dye-job. Too dumb to know not to walk into a crime scene. Do you think she's got a grenade launcher tucked in her cunt?"

"I'll check," the officer who had searched her offered.

At least his companions had the decency to look uncomfortable.

Gwydion grabbed her arm and yanked her away. "Canvas the rest of the building. I'll have someone take her statement."

From the way the others turned away without further argument and headed toward the first locked door, Gwydion probably pushed the suggestion harder than he needed to. Good. Fuck them.

He led Kirby toward the stairs. The instant they were out of sight of the police, he let go of her.

"The fuck was that?" She kept her voice low and walked half a step behind him down the stairs. "Why did they think you were one of them?"

She saw through the illusion. Probably because he refused to use his influence on her.

"Give me your coat." He yanked his hat off and handed it to her.

She narrowed her eyes.

How far did the indoctrination from her childhood run? Would she try to disable him? Kill him? She was still here. Because it didn't matter how many lives he found her through. Even before she remembered who he was, she was always as drawn to him as he was to her.

She shoved her hair under his hat and tugged the brim low over her face. She shrugged out of two layers of clothes, which left her in a long-sleeved top and tattered BDU pants.

That hit too close to home, in regards to their last life together.

They were in the alley behind the building now. The area was empty but wouldn't be for long. She turned to him again. "Why are you—"

"We found the weapon," someone around the corner shouted. "Suspect is still at large."

Which meant Gwydion's excuse of *she's not packing* wouldn't work this time. "Go," he growled.

She hesitated for a heartbeat, and then she was gone in the other direction, finding her way into the sidewalk chaos and vanishing into the crowds.

With her training, she was safer without him. He was a soldier, not an assassin.

He hated watching her go, regardless. He'd find her again soon, but this ranked near the bottom of the list of their first meetings.

STARKAD

Starkad wouldn't pace. He refused. He was ignoring several vital tasks, as well. Like calling the organization. Checking the news. Monitoring police bandwidth.

He couldn't bring himself to do anything until Kirby returned, safe. She could take care of herself, in this life more than in any other, but that didn't stop him from being concerned. If something happened to her, he would tear apart every plane of existence, for vengeance. He was done waiting for Odin's curse to rear its head again. Gods would die by Starkad's hand.

The shadow of silent footsteps appeared under the crack in the door, and every muscle in his body tensed.

Then there was a knock. Not too loud. Not too soft. Three quick, solid raps. A cautious glance through the peephole confirmed it was Kirby.

He composed himself and let her in. A nearly overwhelming urge spilled through him—the same one he felt every time she was around, but more potent than ever—to grip her hair, claim her mouth, and dive into her essence.

He'd gotten good at suppressing that. "I'm glad you're safe," he said plainly.

She brushed past him, jaw clenched, and dropped onto the edge of the bed. She rubbed her face, rather than meeting his gaze. Where did she get the hat? A new flavor of concern joined the blend already growing inside. She could have snagged it from a random place, but three embroidered gold crowns on blue canvas weren't the kind of design one saw every day. The image was King Arthur's crest, and Gwydion had been wearing it for as long as he'd been telling people he'd been the king.

"Ruby?" The nickname was one of the few concessions he allowed himself. It was what he'd called her in her first life, because she was drawn to roses and blood and all things hauntingly, beautifully red.

She finally looked up. "Who's your contact in TOM?"

He'd told her in the past it was safest for everyone if she didn't know. That wasn't a complete lie. If she realized Brit was the one supplying him information, it might break Kirby. More likely though, she'd refuse to comply, and renew her hunt to see her former partner dead. "You know I can't tell you that."

"It was Brit." She spat the name as if it tasted foul. "The team leader on this mission. It was Brit."

"I didn't know. I don't know who's being sent any more than my contact knows you're the one I'm working with." Both true. Brit thought Kirby was dead. It was best that way. "Did she see you?"

"If her spotter is any good at their job, they know it was me. *Fuck.*" Kirby drove her fist into the mattress. "She was right there. A hundred meters away. And I missed her. I fired a fucking flash grenade, and she got away."

And now both women knew about each other. *Fuck* was an understatement. "The target is safe. That's all that matters. You accomplished the primary mission."

"Fuck the primary mission." Kirby was on her feet, doing the pacing Starkad had denied himself. She stalked like a caged cat—graceful, stunning, and deadly. "Okay, so not really. Yay.

Hurray. The target is safe. Now there are TOMs in this city. *Brit.* You heard me say that, right?"

"I get it." He kept his voice calm.

"No. You don't. She betrayed me. I almost died because of her. She said I—" Kirby swallowed hard.

He'd been there, through all of it. He not only understood, he'd also lived centuries of betrayal. Though Kirby had never turned against him, so maybe he didn't completely understand.

"Tell me everything that happened this morning." If he could get her to talk through things, it would force her to think, rather than feel. Years of watching Kirby pull herself back together, after he extracted her from the school, had given him a solid idea of what helped her stay sane.

She paused in the middle of the hotel room and faced him. Anger and hurt flashed in her eyes. She could mask her feelings from almost anyone, but she'd gotten careless with him over time. She recounted the details of her morning, from his call to the TOMs being in the other building, up to finding Brit's AUG.

Starkad wanted to argue that maybe it was someone else's. Even if that was plausible, she wouldn't want to hear it.

"And then there was this guy with the cops. They thought he was one of them." She trailed off, her rage fading.

Well, shit. He'd known Gwydion and Min wouldn't be held off much longer. Of course they'd picked this mission to crash. Because if one of them was here, they both were. An Egyptian god of passion and a Welsh god of… Starkad wasn't even sure what Gwydion was claiming this decade. The situation had gone from *mess* to *dumpster fire*.

"Then what?" Starkad prompted.

Kirby frowned. "Then he told them he was taking my statement, and he helped me get away. I swear I didn't trust him. I didn't give him any information. I went along with it because it was a way out. He didn't follow me."

Starkad wasn't worried about that. Kirby was the best at what she did. His concern was that she felt the need to justify her actions. "I'm glad you're safe. I'll check in. Sit tight until I have our next steps," he said.

"Our next step is finding Brit. I'm going to finish the job." The fire was back in Kirby's voice.

"That's not your call to make. We protect the target. We ensure they're in protective custody. We move to the next location." He stopped himself when she clenched her jaw.

"I work with this organization because they point us in a direction. I don't take orders from anyone. And I didn't think you did either."

If only life were that simple. "We play by their rules because it's how we get what we want." They'd had this fight before. They'd had most of their fights multiple times. "If you want Brit, if you want TOM, you don't piss off the people helping us get them."

Kirby scoffed and shook her head. "She's here now. I want to find her. If she's on her way to the airport. We should be too."

"Are you going to shoot her in the middle of Terminal One?" Starkad asked. "The same day someone blew up a building downtown? Are you going to hop on her flight and pray you can hide yourself for the next couple of hours? From the one person in that organization who's almost as good as you, and who probably knows you're here now?"

If Kirby said *yes*, Starkad would follow. He didn't want it to come to that. *Please let her be reasonable.*

"Fine." She flopped back onto the bed and stared up at the ceiling. "I'll *sit tight*. But I'm hitting the hotel bar, and I'm charging it to the room. Urd can pick up my tab."

"Fine." He would lecture her on being careful, but she had *careful* programmed into her. She'd watch her surroundings. She wouldn't actually drink. And she'd fuck some random stranger.

He hated that last one, but he let it slide. The alternative was telling her why he didn't want her to be with anyone else. Admitting to her that the one thing he wanted more than anything was her.

Kirby pushed to her feet, crossed the room to Starkad, and stopped less than a foot away. She stood so close he could smell the sweat and grime and stress from her morning out, and the hint of desire underneath. She usually hid that better.

"Unless you'd like to be my company for the next couple of hours." She studied him through her eyelashes, her posture abruptly submissive and demure.

He knew exactly what she wanted, because he wanted it too. She wanted him to bind her. Mark her naked flesh. Make her whimper in pain, and then bury himself inside her until she came over and over, and neither of them could think. His cock ached from the suggestion.

She looked like the woman he'd loved. Sounded like her. Moved like her. But until she remembered her past lives, she wasn't his Ruby. She was the girl he'd watched grow from awkward teenager to defiant, stunning woman.

"I have work to do." He had no idea where he found the strength to make his voice hard.

Kirby's sweetness vanished into a sneer. "Great. Have fun doing whatever you do. I'm gonna shower, sleep, and then get laid." She waved over her shoulder and walked out of the room.

If Gwydion and Min were here, she'd start to remember soon. Gwydion had that impact on her. Until then, Starkad would see her stay sane and safe a little longer.

Chapter Eight

6 Years Ago
Kirby

This mission was only recon, but Kirby didn't care. She was finally out in the field. All the training had paid off, and here she was.

Even better, Brit was her spotter. They had their own hotel room, a generous expense account—so they could play the part of the people they pretended to be—and an entire night stretching ahead of them that didn't require them to be anywhere. A movie with lots of explosions and weakly written romance played in the background.

"This. We have to do this." Brit turned her laptop toward Kirby, to show her the screen.

A vast array of sweets, from cake to ice cream to cookies, greeted Kirby. "The only question is, where do we start?"

Brit looked at the screen again. "With the cake. They have a *Party Sampler* that comes with a little of everything."

"There's no way we can eat a party sampler of cake." Though Kirby was willing to try. At home, their diets were as strict as their workout regimen. It was time to take advantage of a new menu.

"Ordering now." Brit's fingers flew across the keyboard.

Being out on their own for the first time wasn't the only reason Kirby was so happy. After what happened in Starkad's class two years ago, when he broke her ankle, it was months before Brit talked to her again. Kirby spent even longer proving that she'd never meant to undermine her. That there was nothing but respect and friendship there.

Nothing but was a little misleading. As Kirby watched Brit now, smiling and ordering cake, fantasy tickled her imagination. Of what it would be like, to crawl across the bed and kiss Brit. To spend hours stripping each other down, exploring Brit's body. Tasting her…

Kirby let the movie play out in the back of her mind but dragged most of her attention from it. One of the classes she'd struggled with was *Seduction*. She was too direct and didn't care for the subtleties of pretending to like someone.

Brit tossed the laptop on the adjoining bed, where it landed with a faint *poof*. "Supposedly, we'll have cake in forty-five minutes."

"I love it. Who knew cake delivery was a thing? I mean, pizza? Okay. Should we get pizza? Do we need dinner, to balance out dessert?"

"Uh… not." Brit screwed her face up in mock disgust. "Next you're going to suggest we have them bring us a salad to go with it."

"I would never." Kirby laughed. The salads at school were the worst. Spinach and kale, swimming in vinegar and oil. Not all the food was bad, but the salads… She could live her entire life happily, never eating another.

She twisted and flopped onto her back on the mattress, so she could lie flat and still see Brit. "What should we do until it gets here?"

They could go over their instructions for tomorrow—building layouts, schedules, streets—but it had all been drilled into their heads, and Kirby could recite the information they had in their sleep. Besides, she wanted space left in her thoughts for whatever they found on reconnaissance.

"Dunno." Brit lay down so her head was next to Kirby's, her body pointed in the other direction. "Seems like we should have a longer list, doesn't it?"

"Kind of." They weren't really deprived in school; they had to know how to function in the outside world. But they weren't able to do anything that didn't fit into an evening's time. Cross-country road trips. Disneyland. Backpacking across Europe.

"Truth or dare?" Brit asked.

Kirby rolled her eyes. "Did you read that in a book? Besides, we already know each other's deep dark secrets."

"Not all of them." Brit scrambled to sit up again. "There are some things we've never shared."

"Did you have something in mind? Something you're dying to get off your chest?"

"Not me. You."

Kirby rolled her head to the side, to study her. "What do I need to confess?" Besides the intense desire she had to be with the woman next to her.

"Hmm…" Brit tapped her chin. "Are you a natural blonde?"

"What?" Kirby had no idea where the question came from, but it was funny. "Pretending you haven't seen me naked in the shower a million times, yes. It's natural. I haven't secretly been bleaching my hair since I was thirteen. That's like me asking you if your lips are really that full and red."

"These?" Brit licked her lips.

Kirby wanted to tilt her head up and do the same.

"Only one way to know for sure." Brit straddled Kirby's waist, dipped her head, and brushed her mouth over Kirby's.

Kirby groaned into the kiss, and lifted her head up to feel more of the soft skin against hers. Tingles raced over her skin. This was nothing like seduction training in school. Every inch of her body hummed with need. No sex she'd had prepared her for the pleasant buzz filling her thoughts, and this was only a kiss.

Brit pulled away with a playful grin but didn't move. "I get another question."

"If I get another kiss." Kirby didn't care if this was just a game. It felt incredible, and she was going to enjoy as much of it as she could get. The ping in her heart argued she did care. But she was willing to ignore that for now.

"That's a trade I'm willing to make," Brit said. "Did you ever fuck any of our teachers?"

Images of Starkad overlapped with those of Brit playing in Kirby's mind. But they were all pretend. "When would I have ever had time for that?"

"You were in the infirmary for a month." She sounded serious.

Kirby stared at her. "No, I haven't fucked any of the teachers. Have you? Who would I have even…? No."

"Me neither." Brit shrugged. "But I heard rumors Starkad came to visit you. He asked to see you alone."

"And he apologized for breaking my foot, but told me I deserved it for making you look bad. You know that."

Brit rested her hands on either side of Kirby's head and kissed her again, lightly enough to tease but not sate. "Did you ever want to?"

"Yes." Kirby had no idea if the answer would ruin the moment. "But so does half of everyone. I'd fuck Chris Evans if he offered, too. That doesn't mean it's going to happen."

Brit kissed her harder this time. Lingering. Gliding her tongue along the seam of Kirby's lips.

Kirby parted her mouth and let her in, diving into the moment. Desire and anticipation flooded her. She could lose herself in this forever. She linked her fingers at the base of Brit's neck, holding her in place and devouring her.

Brit nipped Kirby's bottom lip when she pulled away. "I knew you'd be a Captain America girl." Her lips were bright red and swollen.

Did Kirby look like that? She hoped so. "You say that like it's a bad thing."

"Nope. For you, it's perfect. Kirby the Super Soldier. Created to save the world from irresponsible gods."

Kirby had to admit she liked it. "Think I can get a shield like his?"

"Probably not. But I think your ass would look better in that outfit."

Kirby flushed at the compliment. "I'd have to dye it, though. Can you imagine how much attention I'd draw, wandering the streets in red and white stripes?"

"Maybe everyone would ignore you."

"How do you figure?"

"No one wants to make eye-contact with the nutjob." Brit stuck her tongue out.

Someone knocked, and Kirby's heart jammed in her throat.

"Cake." Brit giggled and climbed off her. "I'll get it."

Right. Kirby couldn't ignore the longing that sank in when Brit's weight was gone. Could they get that moment back?

Brit chatted with the delivery guy for a moment, and locked the door when he left. She half-skipped back with two large boxes and set them on the table. "What do you want to try first?"

"Whatever looks good." Kirby needed to be okay with things if Brit had been fooling around. She couldn't be wounded. She had to wrap up her heart and protect it.

"All of it looks good." Brit looked at the first open box. "Snipp, snapp, snute, du er ute." As she recited a rhyme they'd learned in school, she pointed to a new piece of cake with each syllable. "This'll do." She plunged a plastic knife into the box, then pulled two slices of something chocolate out. "I think this one is strawberries and ganache."

That sounded yummy. Better than yummy. Just the thought of the flavor combination made Kirby's mouth water. She almost swore her nipples tingled. Was she getting turned on by dessert? Or she was still stuck in the need that Brit's teasing filled her with.

Brit handed Kirby a triangle of cake, then settled back onto the bed across from her. "Dig in," Brit said.

The pastry was small enough to take bites from without needing a fork. The flavors melted across Kirby's tongue. It was really good. It was also gone quickly. She licked the extra ganache from the napkin.

Brit laughed.

Kirby fixed her with a playful glare. "I'm not wasting good chocolate."

"And I'm not blaming you. But you have chocolate on your nose."

Kirby scrubbed the side of her hand over her nose, but when she pulled away, her skin was clean. "No I don't."

Brit dipped her finger in her icing and dabbed the results on Kirby's nose. "Now you do."

"You bitch." Kirby flung the retort out without malice.

"Let me," Brit said, grabbing Kirby's wrist before she could wipe the mess away. She leaned in and licked off the chocolate.

Kirby's pulse screamed in her ears. She knotted her fingers in Brit's hair and kissed her. Chocolate and strawberry and repressed desire flitted across Kirby's tongue. She groaned against Brit's mouth and crushed in harder.

Brit raked her nails up Kirby's back and back down. This was incredible. If this was how good the kisses were, what would it be like to feel more? Skin on skin? Naked flesh pressed together? Then again, Kirby was okay with making out for hours, as long as she got to keep touching Brit.

Kirby lost track of time, as their hands roamed each other's bodies and their mouths explored lips and necks and ears. The movie credits were scrolling on the TV.

Brit pulled back with a gasp. "I'm warm. Are you hot?" She trailed her gaze over Kirby. "Dumb question. You're *definitely* hot."

She was now. Heat raced across Kirby's cheeks, mingling with the fire and electricity that flooded the rest of her. "I have the perfect solution." She tugged up the hem of Brit's shirt.

"So smart." Brit yanked off her top, then helped Kirby with hers.

Kirby couldn't help but stare. She was a bit jealous of the practical, plain, white satin that barely restrained Brit's breasts. Her partner was almost spilling out of the large cups. "Gorgeous." Kirby palmed the fleshy mounds and traced her thumbs over Brit's nipples through the fabric.

"You've seen me naked a billion times, and you're impressed with this?" Brit's laughter was punctuated with stuttered gasps.

Kirby kissed along the top of the bra. "This is different. You're different." This was sating the pulse between her thighs and the years of fantasy, and there was no risk here of someone catching them. Telling them this was against the rules.

They continued to explore one another, removing more clothes until the only thing either of them wore was panties.

Brit grabbed Kirby's wrists and pinned her to the bed, straddling her hips. She lowered her head and flicked her tongue over Kirby's nipple. A new jolt raced through Kirby, tugging from her breast to throb in her aching core. Brit wrapped her lips around the swollen nub and sucked, kneading Kirby's other breast at the same time.

Kirby thrust her hips in time to the attention, rubbing her mons against Brit's. The cool air kissed the damp fabric of her panties. Did she want to remove that last barrier to feeling everything? Go all the way? Or was she content to keep teasing and being teased?

Anticipation could be delicious. She wanted Brit to enjoy herself, though. She gripped Brit's hips and rolled them both so she was on top. Brit's delighted giggle was a new kind of alluring.

Kirby kissed a lazy path down Brit's body, to scrape her teeth over the crotch of Brit's panties.

Brit squirmed to get closer, and Kirby pulled away. She hooked her fingers on the elastic and dragged the underwear down Brit's legs. She drew her mouth back up the inside of Brit's thighs, delighting in the warm body squirming under her attention.

When Kirby licked her slit, Brit knotted her fingers in Kirby's hair and bucked her hips into the touch. Kirby's fingers slipped easily along Brit's skin, and she wrapped one on either side of Brit's clit.

Kirby dove into the taste, the sounds, and the warmth pressing into her face. She licked across Brit's clit. Using the moans that greeted her to increase her pace or change her angle.

Brit's gasps became more punctuated. She let out the most delicious cry when she came, grinding into Kirby, holding her in place until she jerked away from the touch.

Need and smugness flowed through Kirby. Her own panties were soaked through with desire. She climbed back up Brit, to crush their mouths together.

"Holy fuck, where did you learn that?" Brit asked breathlessly between desperate kisses.

The question snagged on something in Kirby's mind that she couldn't grasp, and she shoved the thought aside. "I don't know. It just popped into my head."

"I love it when you're inspired." Brit glided her hand down Kirby's stomach and shoved her underwear aside.

At the first brush of fingers along her wet pussy, Kirby arched her back, pressing into Brit's touch.

Brit nudged her back, to suck on one of Kirby's nipples, and teased her hand along Kirby's folds. When she brushed Kirby's clit, a sharp jolt raced through her. Kirby was so close to the edge, it almost sent her tumbling over.

The tiny circles that Brit traced became short strokes.

Kirby humped her hand, focusing on every sensation at the same time, and losing herself in all of it. Orgasm spilled through her, stealing her thoughts and erasing the last of her tension.

Brit eased up as Kirby pulled away, until they both lay on their backs, gasping to catch their breath.

"I didn't think you'd let me do that." Brit spooned against her back.

Kirby would let her do pretty much anything at this point. "Why not?"

"You're Kirby. The unattainable—well—super soldier, who doesn't do anything wrong."

Kirby pressed back into her. "There's nothing wrong about this. Everything is so very right."

"I didn't mean... I thought you weren't interested."

"I was terrified." The confession slipped out without Kirby's permission.

"Of me?"

"Of losing you." She shouldn't admit it, but Brit was her world. This felt like a *now or never* kind of moment. "Of finding out you didn't see me *that way*. Of telling you I love you, and you not saying it back."

"Yeah?"

Kirby glanced over her shoulder, one eyebrow raised.

Brit kissed her bare shoulder. "I love you too. So much."

"After everything I did, when we fought..." The wrong insecurities were slipping out. Kirby needed to stop.

"It doesn't matter. The past is gone, and we have each other now."

Kirby smiled and pulled Brit's arm tighter around her. "We do. And we make a perfect team."

The rest of the mission went as smoothly as Kirby figured recon ever could.

Back home, everything changed, and at the same time, it all stayed the same. Field agents had their own apartments on campus, separate from the students and instructors. Brit spent a lot of nights in Kirby's.

They were careful. Not as much as they could have been, but Kirby didn't think anyone cared. Sure, there was a no-fraternization rule, but the worst anyone had suffered—according to rumors—was a slap on the wrist. Kirby wasn't sure if that was literal. Who knew, in this place?

It was still early enough Brit hadn't snuck back to her room. She'd been tense last night, and Kirby was worried about her, so they spent most of the night cuddling and sharing silly stories.

Someone pounded on Kirby's apartment door. "Lance Corporal Kirby, open up, please."

Chapter Nine

A glance at the clock told Kirby it was barely five in the morning.

Brit was already sitting.

Kirby gave her a quick kiss and whispered, "Stay here. Be right back."

She yanked on pants and a top as quickly as she would have a robe, raked her fingers through her hair, and padded to answer the door.

She recognized the officers on the other side but didn't know their names. They were a few years older than her. Their black shirts and jeans marked them as Campus Security. No one said it to their faces, but everyone knew CS was there because they couldn't cut field work. She raised an eyebrow and waited.

"Both of you, come with us now," they guy in front said.

"Private apartments. I'm the only one here." Kirby glanced over her shoulder. "Do you need your eyes checked?"

The two men in back dropped their hands to holstered stun-guns. The one in front glared. "Someone is at Lance Corporal Brit's place now. When they find it empty, they'll call me."

"And I can't help you with that." Kirby's gut was twisting in on itself. Thank Freya, for her training. "I'll accompany you, though. Do you need directions to the cafeteria?"

"Both of you. *Now*." He shoved a piece of paper at her.

As she unfolded it, the words *Summons* and *Disciplinary Action* glared back at her.

"We're both ready." Brit's voice came from behind.

Kirby swallowed a groan. Without looking, she could picture Brit standing in her bedroom doorway, dressed and at ease. *Fuck.*

Both women followed their escort through the halls. Kirby wanted to lean in and whisper she had this. She'd make everything all right. Unfortunately, there was no option for her to do anything but march with the pack.

They stopped in front of one of the larger meeting rooms, and Kirby's tension cranked higher. This was where the disciplinary board met.

A long table sat at the front of the room, and rows of chairs stretched back toward the door. Hel, Loki, and a few of the instructors were at the table, including Starkad. One chair was singled out directly in front of them, with another to their side.

Hel stood. "Kirby. Approach."

Not Brit? That was a relief. So why did Kirby's gut still feel like it was trapped in a paint shaker? She walked to the front of the room, back straight and expression blank.

"You're accused of assault and coercion of two fellow soldiers, as well as fraternization. How do you answer the charges?"

Guilty on the last one. Shock flooded her over the others. "I absolutely have not engaged in any of those things. And I have the right to face my accuser." A whisper of fear expected Brit to step forward.

When Campus Security opened a side door instead, her relief lasted the half a second it took for Mark to walk into the room.

"Sit, Kirby." Loki gestured to the chair in front of them.

Like some sort of trained dog. *Sounds about right.* She shook the thought aside and did as ordered.

"Lance Corporal Mark, this is Kirby's chance to answer your accusations," Hel said.

Mark took the other free seat and began. His tale started with her first day in school, when she'd attacked him. Except in his version, she was the aggressor. She'd bitten him. Threatened him. Gone to the teachers and blamed him—

"No." Kirby couldn't listen anymore. "Hel was there that first day, and agreed I was right to defend myself. He did those other things to me. When I reported him, I was told to deal with the problem. So I did."

"I never hurt you." Mark looked her in the eye when he told the blatant lie. "And you even went so far as to interrupt one of the classes where I was a student teacher, humiliate me, and injure me."

Kirby clenched her fists. "You threatened me. You groped me. You used sparring time as an excuse to molest and bruise me. And you did it all because you see me as a toy."

"Bruises are a part of training." Hel's voice was hard.

Kirby didn't like the slant of this hearing. It was as if every one of her responses landed in the dead air between her and the front of the room. Was there anything she could say? Should she say nothing? "Not this kind of bruise. Not without intent. And one thing you've most certainly taught us is how to mean the pain we inflict."

Loki's smirk was disconcerting. "Don't blame your shortcomings on others. Why was Lance Corporal Brit in your room this morning?"

"We were discussing strategy." It was getting harder for Kirby to maintain her composure. "We're still learning from our field experiences, and want to take advantage of that knowledge. After hours is when we have time. We're comfortable falling asleep studying."

She was over explaining. She needed to shut up. "I'm good at what I do. I'm the best. Does that mean I should take the blame for Mark's insecurities?"

Loki shook his head. "Being good at what you do doesn't mean you have separate rules, and you're not that great, if you can't accept your own faults."

"I'm not—"

"You don't have the floor," Hel said. "Lance Corporal Brit, approach and take a seat."

Kirby was desperate to look behind her. To watch Brit cross the room. To make some sort of eye contact and get an assurance they were on the same page. She didn't dare.

Brit took Mark's spot, while he moved to the edge of Kirby's vision.

Hel turned to her side. "Brit, what were you doing in Kirby's room this morning?"

"The same thing I've done any other time I've been in her room in the last six months." She met Kirby's gaze. "We fuck."

Kirby was pretty sure her stomach had dropped so far at this point, it had left her body and was in the sub-basement.

"You know that's against the rules." Hel didn't sound surprised.

Brit never looked away. "Kirby does a lot of things that are against the rules."

No.

"The incident with Mark, a few years back. You were in the classroom?"

"I was."

Kirby had tumbled past keeping a stony face and was just praying to not lose her shit and either scream or cry in the middle of the hearing room. What was happening? Brit would tell the truth about Mark, though. She had to.

Kirby didn't like the doubt that said *not likely*.

"The night before the incident, Kirby found me crying in the bathroom." Brit ducked her head. But it was a rehearsed shame, not a genuine response. "I hadn't learned yet that the only way to grow here was to be strong. She tried to take that from me."

What? Was this about the sparring thing, in Starkad's class? They'd moved past that. "That's not what—"

"You're out of line." Loki barked the words. "We'll have you watch remotely if you can't stay silent. Continue, Brit."

"Kirby pursued Mark with the intent of making his life miserable. She sheltered me. She refused to teach, or move aside so I could learn from someone else." Brit's shuddering sigh was too perfectly scripted. "Two years after we met, I wasn't even good enough to spar with her. I'd earned my way into the advanced hand-to-hand classes in spite of her interference, and she told me in front of the entire class that I wasn't worth her time."

This was like some sort of Bizarro universe. Kirby's mind sped to follow the logic and landed on *do they have a point?* No. Kirby had always tried to walk that line between what was best and what kept Brit safe, but she hadn't done any of these things because of jealousy or to keep someone else down.

"She repeatedly humiliated me." Brit wasn't done. Wonderful. "Implied I was second best. Made it her mission to keep me from excelling, so she wouldn't have competition."

"But you have excelled," Hel said.

"And you've been sleeping with her," Loki added.

Brit's laugh was bitter. "Of course I have. When the golden child on campus says, *do this or life gets worse*, you don't tell her *no*."

Oh gods. Kirby's heart fractured and crumbled. None of what they shared was real. "I was protecting you. I was helping you. I love you."

"You took advantage of me." Brit's hard voice wasn't an act.

Kirby's mind twirled and tumbled and unraveled.

"You used your position. Your power. I've never had a choice but to tell you *yes*."

How had Kirby seen the last few years so differently? Had she pushed Brit into this? Was Kirby so delusional she never realized what she was doing?

"I don't love you." Brit turned to Hel. "She's a fucking monster. Worse than those we hunt. I'm terrified every time I'm alone with her."

"Enough." Hel slammed her palms onto the table. "Standing strong is one thing. Manipulation is not our realm."

Kirby wanted to argue it was Loki's, but mostly because his wrath would be easier to face than what Brit said.

"Kirby's never exhibited any of these behaviors anywhere else," Starkad said "She's treated like the best because she is the best."

She would have sobbed with relief that someone came to her defense, if her insides hadn't already shattered.

Hel regarded Starkad for a moment, then said, "You know as well as all of us that how an individual acts in public is not a reflection of who they are. You recognized the issue, or you wouldn't have taken corrective action in your class the way you did."

Starkad winced.

Hel continued. "I've heard enough. Kirby, we're demoting you back to Cadet. You're no longer a field agent, and you're on probation. You'll be given an administrative assignment. When you leave your room, you'll do so with Campus Security. You'll stay away from Brit and Mark. Your position will be re-evaluated in six months."

As the words rolled off Hel's tongue, they encased Kirby's disbelief in stone. There was no point in feeling or reacting. This outcome was decided before she arrived. Her hearing was all for show.

Kirby nodded and thanked the hearing committee, because what else could she do? She fell into step with her Campus Security escorts back to her room, and listened as they locked her inside.

She sat on her bed and stared at the wall and tried to forget that a few short hours ago, she'd lain under those sheets with Brit, thinking they both felt the same kind of love for each other.

The incidents discussed in her hearing played through her head in vivid splashes. Memories of the way Mark tormented her in private—the cruel words, the hidden marks… She remembered falling for Brit. Her doubt. Her fear. Her exhilaration when Brit made the first move.

Was Kirby to blame for Mark's cruelty? She'd made him look bad her first day in school. But… was she supposed to roll over and take it? She didn't do that. No one here did that.

And with Brit, she never…

Had Kirby been wrong to help her? That didn't make sense.

None of it mattered. Kirby's reputation wouldn't recover from this. The charges were the kind of stain that would never vanish. She'd wasted her training. She wasn't a sniper anymore. She wasn't anything.

Kirby had knowledge to share. But they didn't want her doing that. If her crime was abusing her position, they'd never let her teach again.

Brit's words cut the deepest. The disdain. The fake despair. The coldness in her eyes whenever she looked at Kirby.

The hearing went round and round in her mind, the accusations growing louder and her own will to argue falling farther away with each circuit. The memories clawed and mutated as she slipped into a pit. The only thing waiting for her that far down was Mark. Molesting her. Tormenting her. Threatening her.

And Brit, telling the world that Kirby destroyed her life.

The loop sped up and slowed down and nauseated her, but it never stopped. She didn't realize the entire day had passed, until she looked at her clock. Almost twelve hours since the knock on her door. Since her world was ripped away from her.

Since the only woman she loved and the only thing she cared about were ripped away from her.

She should take a shower. See about… getting on with life? If she asked one of her guards to bring her dinner, would he? After the way she'd treated Campus Security, she might wish he hadn't. Now she wasn't even worthy of licking their boots.

The bright white of the bathroom lights was harsh on her eyes. It gleamed in the mirror, but the last thing she wanted to see was her own face. The light glinted off a razor lying near the sink. She'd shaved pretty much everything before Brit came over yesterday, and meant to throw away the old blade when she was done.

Brightness danced off the flat surface and the sharp edge, captivating her. Such a simple little thing, capable of doing so much. Made to be discarded when it was no longer useful.

Just like Kirby.

The thought clenched like a fist around her lungs until she struggled to breath. She gripped the edge of the counter, staring at the way the corner bit into her palms. She pressed in more and more of her weight. Nothing happened. Nothing satisfying, anyway. The dull ache in her elbows was an irritation at most.

She picked up the razor and turned it this way and that, casting spots of white on the walls and ceiling. She pressed the edge to her fingertip. A stark drop of red welled up, and the sting raced through her nerves. It wasn't a lot of pain, but it dragged her away from her spiraling thoughts. That was nice.

The instant she recognized the mental frustration was gone, it rushed back. She needed it to stay away. Had to find a way to keep herself out of her own mind.

She dragged the blade along the fleshy pad of her palm, in the crease left by the countertop, and gasped at the pain. It was a bad spot to injure, but it didn't matter. She wasn't going to be using her hands for anything intensive for a few months. Or ever again.

Mark and Brit took that from her.

Or Kirby brought this on herself. All this time, she thought she was being strong. Turned out she was weaker than anyone. Not seeing the signs of what was going on around her. Thinking Brit loved her.

A drop of blood fell to the floor with a silent *splash*. She needed to do this in the shower, to make cleanup easier when she was done.

She stepped into the small tile enclosure, still clothed. If the cut on her hand wasn't enough to keep her from thinking, she needed more. A deeper, more intense pain.

She dragged the blade down the inside of her wrist. It took all of her restraint to keep from crying out, but at least she'd learned that lesson early in life. Cry in private. Bleed in silence. Never let them see any weakness. That was her mistake—she let Mark and Brit see that her strength was a front.

This was better, though. The dark red streaming down her skin was pretty. Thick. Fluid.

The room around her titled and spun, and she sank to the ground. She needed to wash away the mess and clean up.

In a minute. Once the haze cleared from her head.

Or never again.

Never waking up sounded even better.

CHAPTER TEN

6 YEARS AGO
STARKAD

As one of her mentors, Starkad participated in Kirby's review. He wasn't surprised that no one else spoke on her behalf. He'd been at odds with the other gods and berserkers for centuries—long before TOM existed—and didn't give a shit what they thought. She hadn't done the things she was accused of. The one thing she was guilty of was never learning to hide her affection for Brit.

His heart cracked on Kirby's behalf when Brit made her accusations. He felt and shared her rage when Mark spoke and Brit agreed with him.

And he wanted to put a fist through someone when Kirby was stripped of her rank and team-leader status, placed on probation, and assigned to an office job. She was forbidden from field assignments, teaching, or even using the practice rooms when anyone else was in them. She wasn't allowed to interact in private with cadets. The only one-on-one she could have was with instructors.

And in a few months, they'd re-evaluate her behavior.

By the time they finished explaining her sentence, she might as well have been made of marble. She didn't meet anyone's gaze. She stared straight ahead and stalked from the room.

Starkad let her go. Regardless of how he felt about her past incarnations, he'd kept his distance here. She was a student and nothing more. No one here knew there was a reason for him to reach out and offer comfort or advice.

He went back to his own room and tried to lose himself in his evening routine. Ill ease sat heavy in his heart. The more he worked to distract himself, the stronger the bad feeling got.

Something was wrong with Kirby. More than a dozen lifetimes, and he'd known each time, right before she died. It felt like having his soul sucked from his bones.

This wasn't as potent, but it was bad.

He headed to her room, master key in hand. He hated that staff had this means of entering student rooms, but tonight he was grateful.

Campus security stood guard at her place. How did he forget that? Hel must be awfully confident in how badly beaten down Kirby was, to only post one person.

"Take a walk," Starkad said.

"Sir?"

"Fifteen minutes. Go get a cup of coffee. You've got a long night ahead of you."

The guard hesitated. When Starkad raise an eyebrow, the guard said, "Yes, sir," and walked away.

If the rest of this venture went even half as easily, Starkad would consider swearing loyalty to Odin again.

Kirby didn't answer when he knocked. It could be because she was upset. He hammered on the door with the side of his fist, trying to express urgency without drawing other attention.

Still no answer, and the clawing in his veins was becoming unbearable. He unlocked her door and stepped inside.

Her living room and bedroom were empty. She was nowhere to be found.

The bathroom door sat ajar, light spilling around the cracks.

He nudged the door open wider.

Kirby was slumped against the shower wall, blood caked heavy on her wrists and soaking her jeans.

Fuck. "Kirby." He crossed the room in two steps and grabbed a towel from the rack. "Please be all right." He didn't care who heard his prayer— gods, demons, mischief incarnate—as long as she survived.

He applied pressure to the wounds with one hand, while he felt for a pulse with the other. Her breathing was shallow and her heartbeat faint, but she was alive.

The towel wasn't going to cut it. The only silver lining he saw in this heavy black cloud was that everyone had full first-aid kits in their cabinets. He'd worry about sterilization later. Right now, he needed to seal the wounds and get her out of this fucking place. He wrapped her wrists tightly with gauze, scooped her into his arms, and carried her from the room.

There was no one in the hallways. Another small miracle to be grateful for. She felt so light. It was true, he was strong, but a part of his head insisted this was because she'd lost so much blood.

Starkad brought her to his car and laid her in the back seat. He covered and secured her as best he could, and drove from the grounds. Someone with actual medical training needed to examine her. He'd call Gwydion, except the god wasn't local. Also, Gwydion would find a way to kill Starkad over something like this, if Kirby didn't survive.

No. There was no such *if.* Kirby would make it out of this. There were no other options. He wouldn't lose her. As he drove, he called a friend and asked Dr. Dan Nichols to meet him at his destination. He gave the briefest details. She'd slit her wrists. She'd lost a lot of blood. Any work they did on her had to be at Starkad's place.

Rather, it was Min's. The god owned property around the world, and used a lot of it as safe houses for the organization that was trying to stop TOM. Min had a small house here *just in case.* Starkad had prayed they'd never have to use it. Lot of good that had done him.

"I can't do blood transfusions outside the hospital," Dan said.

"If it comes to that, we'll figure it out." Starkad would move mountains to keep Kirby alive.

Using a couple of TOM connections to get a compatible blood type was nothing. It didn't matter how many bridges he burned tonight; he'd save Kirby. He'd protect her.

How did he let things go this far?

The doctor arrived just a few minutes after Starkad carried Kirby to a room.

Few words were exchanged as Dan went to work. Starkad lingered a few feet away the entire time, concern and prayer rolling through him.

Finally, Dan stood and stepped back. "She'll live. She doesn't need blood, but she does need rest and sugar. And"—he looked between her and Starkad—"there are a lot of things I'll do for you, but she looks a little young…"

"She's an adult, and it's not like that. She's a student who needs help."

Dan knew Starkad taught, and that the details were questionable beyond that. Starkad was grateful he didn't push for more information. Dr. Nichols pulled a blister pack from his bag and handed it over. "Sedatives. Don't leave her alone. Get her a psych eval. Do you need me to bring you anything?"

"I'll have something delivered. How soon can I move her?" They couldn't stay in town for long. TOM would be looking for her, and there were only so many places he could hide, locally.

"She needs to rest as much as possible."

"It may not be safe to keep her here."

Dan sighed. "Give her a day to sleep. Make sure wherever she is, she's comfortable. This is as much for her mental health as anything."

"Will do." Starkad had to walk that line between recovery and hiding.

The doctor left, and came back a few minutes later with a few sodas and candy bars from the vending machine. "Call me if you need anything."

"Thank you." Starkad slipped him some money and sent him on his way. He knelt on the floor next to the bed and brushed Kirby's hair from her forehead. She was so pale, she almost vanished into the pillowcase. "I'm sorry," he said softly. "I knew you'd face worse than a broken ankle, but if I'd had any idea this was a potential outcome…" What? Would he have done things differently?

There was no way to change the past. A lesson he'd lived too many times. The only option now was to make sure she survived to appreciate the future. He sat next to her all night. Sometimes she'd stir and almost focus on him. A couple of times she asked for water, and he obliged.

Mostly, she slept.

Her eyelids fluttered, and he was alert in an instant.

"I'm cold," Kirby said.

Starkad grabbed the comforter from the other bed and draped it over her. "This should help." He expected her to fall asleep again, like she'd been doing.

"You saved me, didn't you? Why?" She watched him with sad eyes.

Because he loved her. Because he'd never been able to save her before. "Because it was the right thing to do."

Her harsh laugh startled him. "We don't do what's *right*. We do what we're told. And I didn't want to be saved. What made you think you deserved to make that choice for me?'

"You made your decision, I made mine." He'd expected curiosity, possibly even concern or mistrust, about why he'd singled her out above everyone else. Anger over saving her life was something he didn't know how to deal with.

She sat and pulled all the blankets around her. "Not a good enough reason."

"It's the only one I've got. When you feel up for it, we need to leave. TOM will find us."

"They can have me. They took everything else already. They can crucify me, for all I care. TOM stole my fucking life. I don't deserve to take the pathetic strands that are left and spend the next few months cowering, until they hunt me down."

He didn't know how to deal with the despair and resignation in her voice. "The feeling will pass. Until then, you shouldn't be making any decisions."

"Really? *Really?*" Bitterness filled her question. "The only reason to leave would be to have the freedom to finally make my own decisions. I finally did, too. I chose to leave this world. I wanted it. I acted on it. And you took that from me."

"Kirby."

"*Leave me the fuck alone,*" she screamed.

He nodded and walked out of the room. He wasn't surprised when the door slammed behind him.

Starkad would give her time, but that didn't mean he'd drop his guard. He'd spent centuries waiting. He could sit in the living room, ears strained, to make sure she didn't try anything like what she had last night.

The candy bars and soda were by her bed. He hoped she ate. He ordered takeout. When it arrived, he knocked and left the food in front of her door.

A few minutes later, the door cracked, and the food vanished inside.

And he waited some more. It was dark again when she emerged. She had her arms wrapped around herself, and misery was painted on her face.

"Thank you for saving me." Her voice was soft.

"I'm sorry I didn't do it sooner."

"I don't understand why you did it."

"Because you deserved—deserve—better." He had to leave the answer at that. Going into detail tonight would as likely make things worse as help.

Kirby hugged herself tight and lingered at the edge of the room. This wasn't the little girl they inducted into TOM. This woman wore the same face as his Ruby, as she stood in front of him, looking like she'd never find her way again.

A fist squeezed around his chest. If they were still student and teacher, every bit of this would cross a line. But they weren't, and he wasn't going to fuck her, just comfort a soul that needed a direction.

"Come here," he said.

Somehow she made trudging across carpet look graceful. When she was close, he pulled her into his lap and wrapped his arms around her.

Kirby leaned into his chest. She didn't cry or shake. She just sat there, breathing even. Had she fallen asleep again?

"How did you know to find me?" she asked, startling him.

There were so many things he had to wait to tell her, and some he didn't know if he ever could. But this one, he could be honest about. "I had a feeling, so I went to check on you."

"And we need to leave?"

"Unless you want to go back. I'd rather you didn't, but it's your choice."

"I'm nothing without that place. And Brit—" She choked on a sob that racked her whole body. "I'm not anything on the outside."

"You're so very much the opposite." It would take time for him to prove it to her, but he would, given the chance.

She pulled away to look him in the eye. "Will they really come after us?"

"No one walks away from TOM."

"What happens when they find us?"

"I'll make sure they never do." Starkad had hidden from the gods before. He could do it again without breaking a sweat. Especially to keep Kirby safe.

She extracted herself from his lap. "All right. Let's go."

He said a quick prayer to any god who might hear him that she'd be all right. Physically, she'd recover. If he'd broken her mentally, by keeping her in that place for so many years, he'd never forgive himself.

Chapter Eleven

Now
Kirby

Kirby sat on the edge of her bed, fists clenched, as she stared at the carpet. Brit was here. Same small city. Living her life. Doing her duty to her gods. Killing. Not caring.

Did Brit look back with pride on what she'd done to Kirby, or had she forgotten the betrayal? Which would be worse?

Starkad's brushing Kirby off hurt the most. Not his turning down her suggestion of sex—that was expected. But pretending Brit being here was the same as any other TOM? And there was that flash in his eyes when she said Brit's name. He knew something, and he wasn't talking.

She should go anyway. She could find Brit. Sure, she'd promised to wait, but she'd broken promises and rules before.

And always regretted it. Not *always*. There was one of his rules she wouldn't hesitate to break again. She was only sorry he hadn't taken her up on it.

Kirby's past was littered with plenty of mistakes she needed to learn from. She should ignore her instinct and stay put. She didn't actually plan on charging expensive drinks to the room, but she could play the overpriced pay-per-fifteen-minutes videogame system hooked up to the TV.

An hour of dying on Level One because she couldn't get Brit's smug face out of her head convinced her to do something else. She shut the system down.

Maybe a shower would help her relax. She stripped down, and stepped under the hot jets. One of her favorite things about hotels had always been the unlimited hot water.

Water poured over her, beating heat into her skin and washing away the morning's grime. She closed her eyes and pressed her forehead to the cool tile, to lose herself in the contrasting temperatures.

"She took advantage of me." Brit's voice flashed in her thoughts, as loud and vivid as if the other woman was standing next to her.

Kirby's gut churned, and bile rose in her throat.

"She used her position of power. I couldn't say no. *What was I supposed to do?"*

Kirby bit the side of her fist, to smother a frustrated scream.

"I don't love her. She's a fucking monster. I'm terrified every time I'm alone with her."

Kirby wasn't any of those things.

Unless I am.

This voice was her own. And it was a lying fucking bitch.

Just because I don't like it doesn't make it a lie. They raised me to be a killer. I'm the best. I don't have any moral high ground.

She was tracking down all of TOM's other killers. Why did she exempt herself? No. She refused to slide into that pit. The voice that lived in that darkness could stay tucked away in the dark corner of her soul. Kirby had fought hard to keep it at bay. Starkad helped.

He doesn't want me either.

That was different. And if she asked him to be here for this, he would be. Walk out of her room and a few doors down, to him. Ask him to help her stay grounded. He'd do that without hesitation.

But he won't fuck me.

She wouldn't emotionally blackmail her way into his bed. And she wouldn't let him see her backslide like this.

Because I'm weak. Because I can't deal with what life handed me. Because I use excuse after excuse, to pretend I deserve a life.

Kirby recognized the lies. A tiny part of her tried to scream *don't listen*, but the other voice was louder. She had razors in her suitcase. She was only supposed to use her electric razor.

It wasn't as though Starkad would spank her if he found out. And at this point, his *I'm very disappointed in you* would be an extra reason to hate herself. Besides, Kirby wasn't going to use them.

Then why do I keep them?

She wouldn't kill herself, or anything so drastic. A few tiny cuts along her chest, where they'd hurt like hell but not interfere with her work, and she could shock herself out of her own head.

Kirby knotted her fingers in her wet hair, and another scream bubbled up in her throat. The last thing she needed was someone coming to check on a shouting woman. She clenched her jaw, swallowing the frustration and squeezing her eyes shut until tears leaked out the sides.

I have to do something. I need the pain to stop.

She pressed her palms to the shower wall and leaned her weight into them. She couldn't see the pale white scars on her wrists, but she knew they were there. She kept the cutting scars hidden, but the failed suicide marks were there to remind her. To make sure she never forgot how low she sank after Brit...

Kirby choked on a sob.

Kirby needed to get out of here and surround herself. Maybe people-watch. Being in public would force her to stay on alert. She hoped.

She finished showering, then dried off and yanked a sundress on. She was getting laid, and she needed something that was easy to get in and out of. She shouldn't head out as herself. A wig was the last thing she wanted to put on. The blue cap with the three crowns sat harmlessly on the nightstand—one of the few things in the room that didn't call to her tortured past. It was a horrid accessory for her outfit. She didn't give a fuck.

I'm so pathetic.

She whimpered through clenched teeth. She yanked on the hat, grabbed her room key and a fresh set of ID from the lining of her suitcase, and headed down to the hotel bar.

It was three in the afternoon. The bartender and a waitress were the only people here. That didn't mean Kirby could let her guard down, and she was grateful for that. She picked a table in the back corner, away from any windows and with a clear view of all the entrances.

The waitress stood at the bar, one foot hooked on the rung running around the bottom, and twirled a strand of hair around her finger. She was eating up the bartender's story about how he'd been near the explosion this morning.

"Oh my God. I would have died, I'd be so scared." Her tone was exaggerated.

So was the bulge in his slacks—sock stuffed down there, for sure. Kirby shouldn't have been able to see it from here, but somehow he'd managed to raise himself high enough to look casual about showing it off.

She turned her attention to the TV. This morning's incident made national news. Wonderful. Seeing fifty gazillion cell-phone recaps of the madness was exactly what she needed. Not. As soon as she saw, *Police haven't identified any suspects at this time*, she turned her attention from the closed captions.

Since both she and Brit had survived, either TOM or Urd would have a scapegoat in place in a few days. They'd attach this to someone else, who'd been recently arrested. Both groups kept tabs on a frighteningly high number of people. There were pre-built solutions in place, for any incident like this.

This wasn't the distraction Kirby hoped for. *I could head back to my room. I just need a little relief. It's not like it's a big deal.*

She grabbed the drink menu instead, and stared at the bizarrely named options. At least half of them were alcohol free. Which was good. Alcohol hindered her reactions. A sugar addiction would be a nice change from her relationship with pain. She ordered a Tahitian Coffee. The first sip made her wince. Lime and cold brew weren't meant to be together. But once the flavors settled on her tongue, she downed the rest of it quickly.

What next? Focusing on the ridiculous flavor combinations was the perfect distraction. Mango Mule… that was tempting. It probably didn't live up to lime and coffee, though. She had expectations now.

I don't want this. Who am I fooling? I want to be alone. There's a much faster way to get my fix.

Her skin begged for that sharp, fast slice of steel. The release that came with it. The euphoria of pain when she cut her skin.

The soul-devouring self-loathing that came after—Kirby needed more of that. A giant pit to sink into. She didn't even know if she was being sarcastic.

Starkad would help.

He doesn't want to put up with my shit. He's sick of me, throwing myself at him. He helps me out of some misguided sense of obligation—

That wasn't true. He was kind. *He's cruel.* He brought pleasure. *Through pain.* Which was exactly what she needed right now.

If she closed her eyes, she could feel the sting of his belt on her skin. Hear his deep growl in her ear. He could offer a welcome release.

Too bad I burned that bridge.

And there was no one in the bar, let alone someone worth hooking up with. Bartender with the sock-cock didn't count.

"I like your hat." The familiar voice startled her.

She jerked her head up to find the man who'd rescued her from the police standing next to her table. He was as breathtaking now as he had been a few hours ago. Strawberry blond hair that brushed his ears, piercing green eyes that reflected a sadness she felt in her bones, and smile that made her heart skip. How did he approach without her knowing? Even distracted, she should have seen him. Her blood ran like ice through her veins, shoving aside the burst of attraction.

"For as long as you've been staring at that drink menu, has it revealed the secrets of the universe to you?" he asked.

Her pulse hammered in her ears, and her skin was cold. She needed to go now. Every inch of her body screamed *leave*. The flutter in her chest said *stay*.

What the fuck? She was self-destructive, but not on that level. She stood.

He grabbed her wrist.

Instinct kicked in. She needed to twist free. Knee him in the balls. Walk away before she drew more attention.

She couldn't wrench from his grip. His fingers were like a steel vice.

Kinda hot.

Not the time. If she cut through the back halls, she could duck in the women's room. If he hesitated at all to follow her, it would give her time to slip out. If that didn't make him take pause, she was cornered.

Which way could she run? Front desk? Sock-cock bartender?

"This is usually the part where you tell your brain to shut the fuck up, and listen to what your heart and body want." He sounded like he was discussing mild weather.

Usually? Everything about this was wrong. Except that her heart *was* still begging her to stay. On each rapid-fire beat, to the point it was drilling into her thoughts. *Don't go. Don't go. Don't go.*

"Let go of me, or I'll scream. How well does the trick you played on the cops work if people already think you're the bad guy?"

He raised an eyebrow.

How did she know that had been a trick of his, or how it worked this morning? She wasn't sure, but it was one thing her mind and body agreed on. He could only influence certain people, in certain states of mind. Was it something she'd learned in school?

He dropped her wrist. "If you leave, I won't give you answers."

"I'm calling your bluff—that's not the way to get me to stay." Except she was still here. "If you have to bribe me with information, I don't have a way to know if you're lying."

"You'd know, and I'm not bribing you or blackmailing you or trying to trick you. However, I do refuse to shout at your retreating back."

If Kirby wasn't going to walk away—the only thing she should be considering—she should at least use the voice commands programmed into her phone, to let Starkad know she was in trouble. "And if I stay, you'll spoon-feed me half-truths that are vague and unhelpful, and each time I ask for more, you'll have another requirement for me to meet?"

He frowned. "You watch too many cop movies. How about I hand you my wallet?"

"Not sure what good that's going to do." Curiosity was winning out. Probably because it was tainted with a heavy dose of self-destruction. *I wanted a hookup. He's hot.*

And now her mind was filled with images of her, wrapping her legs around his waist. Feeling his hot breath on her neck. On her pussy.

Seriously. What the fuck was wrong with her? Starkad would say her problem was recklessness plus self-destruction, mixed with a heavy dose of horniness. And once again, he'd be right.

"Will your ID have your real name on it?" she asked.

"It doesn't. It has the name I've been using for the last… little while. But it also has my credit cards and room key, so I'm highly inconvenienced if you take my wallet and leave."

"Who are you?" She shouldn't care.

He gestured to the chairs. "Sit, and I'll tell you."

"Nope. That's a condition. I met the *stay and listen* one. Give me something in return. Besides a wallet with someone else's name on everything."

"My name is Gwydion. I'm—"

"A Welsh trickster god." Her mouth spit out the words before her brain caught up. As trickster gods went, she very much preferred this one's history over Loki's. "Gwydion is also a god of art and a local hero." That was why she was familiar with how he'd fooled the cops earlier. He was on the curriculum when she was growing up, because TOM hated him. Bonus point in his favor, and a reason to give him a couple more minutes.

No part of her argued he might be lying. It wasn't common knowledge that gods walked among people, so for him to pick an obscure one, who just happened to be capable of what he'd done earlier, and hope she would believe such a ludicrous story… If he was lying, his thought process was still fascinating.

She sat.

Besides, if he kept being charming and reasonable, she could fuck him, and if he turned out to be a vengeful god, at least she'd die fighting. "If you're going to kill me, what are the odds you'll make it fast?"

He searched her face, sadness heavy in his green eyes.

Her heart cracked at the sight. Why?

"I'm not going to kill you." He sounded sincere. He could be lying anyway, especially since he looked like he'd wanted to say something else.

Chapter Twelve

Gwydion

I'd give my heart and soul and power and entire existence, to keep you from dying again. That was what Gwydion wanted to say. *I'm not going to kill you,* sounded far less obsessive.

Though, revealing his true name and nature was far easier this life than it had been in others. Perhaps letting Starkad raise her among gods wasn't all bad. This was also the first time she'd ever gotten the pronunciation of Gwydion's name right on the first try. Like *Gideon,* but with a soft *w* after the *g.*

In each of her lives, something was different about her. Her experiences shaped who she became, until—*if*—she remembered her pasts. But this Kirby… He recognized her body, but not her attitude. He'd never said that before.

That didn't make him want her any less. Desire snaked over his skin, humming with memories. And he wanted to know what had hurt her in this life. The whispers of pain in her eyes were new. Her reluctance to hear Gwydion out was new. And with her on edge like this, introducing her to Min was a bad idea. She was always on her guard when she first met Min. His all-consuming passion for her was intimidating from the outside looking in.

Not that Gwydion would be able to call him off.

"Why did you help me this morning?" Kirby asked.

Gwydion took the chair across from her. He hadn't seen her pull the trigger. He wasn't supposed to know who she was or what she was involved in. He was also incapable of lying to her. "I was walking through town, I saw an explosion, and I was curious. I followed it. The thing about being a god is that life rarely holds surprises. Flash-bang grenade in the middle of Salt Lake City, during morning rush hour? That's surprising."

"How do you know what kind of explosion it was?" Her back was ramrod straight, and her gaze was fixed on his face.

If he were a god of passion, or a berserker with a mildly heightened sense of smell, he might know if her body was as aroused as his. Every inch of his skin burned with a need to refresh the past. He hated fighting the desire to crush his mouth to hers. "Another thing about being as old as I am—I've seen a lot of people die. A lot of them because they did stupid things, but not all. Most of the gods say *fuck it*. I can't look the other way."

"Kind of you. Not relevant, but possibly endearing."

He gave her a dry smile. "So whenever my fragile little heart can tolerate it, I'm an army doctor. Last enlistment was the Gulf War." Where he'd met Kirby in her most recent life. Those memories were potent. Less than thirty years had passed. Barely a heartbeat. And he'd had so many glorious months with her. "I've been on the front line for centuries. I know what a warzone looks like, urban or otherwise."

She raised her eyebrows. If this was the woman he knew, she believed him. He wished he could say that was true here.

"I told you I'd give you answers," he said.

"But you also avoided my first question. Why did you help me?"

He had to measure his words. "That cop was an asshole. You obviously weren't the owner of that AUG, and taking their attention off you, letting you walk away, meant they could focus on the real suspects."

She narrowed her eyes. She'd heard the half-truth. He braced himself for her to walk away for the second time today.

"I'm sorry to interrupt," Min said from behind Gwydion.

Well, fuck. Kirby was going to bolt now, for sure.

KIRBY

Kirby was going a new flavor of nuts. She must be. She came down here to ignore the mental voices. To talk herself out of going after Brit without prep or intel. To keep herself from cutting…

And now she was staring at this stranger—a fucking god, which made him untrustworthy by nature—and fantasizing about screwing him in fifty different ways. When he said *army doctor*, she had the most vivid, intense flash of him taking her on an exam table. She swore she could feel the latex gloves on her skin.

If she was going to go insane, this was a far more pleasant way than the path her mind was on earlier. She should listen to her instinct. Fucking was a good way to reset the brain. They even taught that in school.

Nope. She was still insane.

Then someone else approached. She'd seen the tall, broad-shouldered, ebony-skinned man enter the dining room. A new impulse teased her—the desire to climb into his lap and drag her fingertips over his buzzed hair, until he claimed her. He set off every alarm in her skull. Her body, on the other hand, hummed ever louder with arousal, and all either man had done was look at her.

Like she was the most precious thing in the universe.

"Are you a god too?" she asked the new arrival. How did she know that? If it was true, what did gods want with her?

What do gods always want? To use me.

"I am." He extended his hand. "Min."

She didn't know this one. He must not register on TOM's threat- or ally-scale. "Karen." At least she had the presence of mind to not give them her real name. When she gripped his hand, fissures of desire sped over and through her veins.

She swallowed a whimper. She was everything Starkad accused her of. Reckless. Self-destructive. She didn't care. Not at this moment. If they were gods, they could snap her without hesitation.

Or they could break her in the most delicious way possible. She couldn't drink. She *could* fuck. Ride that high of endorphins. Her life might not depend on it, but her sanity did. Not that they'd offered, but it was early.

Kirby toed out the chair nearest Min.

He accepted the invitation and sat like the mass-produced wooden seat was a throne.

"And what are you a god of, Min?" Kirby asked.

"Passion." The word rolled off his tongue like silk sliding over her skin. "Life. Love. Exploration."

Pleasant shivers glided down her spine, mingling with the hint of fear she'd tasted when he approached. That last bit was the perfect amount of spice. Was he in her head, amplifying her desires? There were limits even to her self-destruction. If she was going to tumble into a pit of vipers, she was doing it of her own accord. "Are you influencing me right now?" If he was, it was similar to the trick Gwydion pulled with the police officers, but instead of changing Min's appearance, it drove lust straight to her core.

Min quirked an eyebrow. *"Influencing? You're quite direct, aren't you?"*

"When the situation calls for it."

She didn't miss the smirk that played on Gwydion's face. That was sexy.

"I'm not *influencing* you," Min said. "Any deep, intense, carnal cravings you feel are your own." He could be lying. Each time he spoke, she swore his tongue glided along the inside of her ear, whispering the words.

She could still think, though. Not that she was listening to herself, but if he was trying to convince her of something, he'd erase her doubt, wouldn't he? "I never said anything about carnal cravings."

"I'm a god of passion. Unless you're concerned I might *influence* you to live."

A lump lodged in her chest, and a ghost ache stung in her wrists. That hit too close to home. Time to change the subject. "Do you two know each other?"

"Sure. We hang out in the god club together. Play Texas Hold 'em on Tuesday nights. Never play strip poker with this guy. He likes to lose." Gwydion winked and nodded at Min.

A snort of laughter slipped out before Kirby could stop it. "You say that like it's a bad thing."

"He only pretends to be intimidated by me." Min leaned in. "Tell me, my huntress. What kind of woman doesn't bat an eye at being approached by two men who say they're gods?"

The kind who was raised to kill the next generation of immortals. "Would you believe me if I said I've got that much spare faith to go around?"

"Would you bend yourself over my knee if I told you I spank little girls who lie to me?" Min countered.

Kirby's imagination plummeted into the gutter, where she not only bent herself over, but she was also willingly bare-assed and begging him to use her when he was done. *Fucking hell*, she needed to get laid. But she wasn't impressed by any asshole who thought he was owed her submission just because he demanded it. Especially with the rapid shift from casual conversation to ass-slapping. "Is this where you order me back to your room, so you can teach me how a good girl behaves?"

"Never. This is where I earn your trust and respect, so I'm worthy of taking you back to my room. As for teaching… I don't do that. I want you comfortable with the rules before we play," Min said.

Gwydion leaned in, mouth near her ear. "You don't have to respect me first, as long as we both have fun." His tone was playful.

She hid her amusement better this time. "How much trust is possible if we're all keeping secrets?"

"As much as you give to any stranger you won't tell your real name." Min's reply tugged at that same thread of fear inside. The one he evoked by being here.

It was probably the best and worst response she could have. Her body was humming a lovely *you only live once* tune. "None of them have been gods."

"And yet, you're still here." Each time Min looked her over, another spike of heat flooded her body. But it was more than that. It was as though his dark gaze called directly to her soul.

"Maybe I'm hoping for at least a little seduction."

Gwydion tapped the brim of the hat she wore. The one he'd given her. "Maybe this was never about seduction, and I just wanted to compliment you on your crown."

"This is where you listen to what your heart and body want." Kirby recited his earlier response back at him. Not the whole thing, because the *usually* had her asking more questions than she was comfortable with. "There's a lot more innuendo in those words than *nice hat.*"

He grinned. "Fair point."

"Would you like to be wooed and seduced?" Min grazed his fingers along the back of her arm. His voice was deep and hypnotic. "I'll tell you how stunning you are. How fierce and beautiful. That the sun rises on your smile and sets with your grief. That the ocean can't compete with the vast potential I see in your eyes. That the finest porcelain could never compare to your skin. I'll kneel at your feet and worship you until you sing. I'll bathe you in oil and shower you in rose petals. I can tell you all of that, and you'll know I mean every word. But you still won't trust it or me."

"That's a bit over the top." But the compliments warmed her to her core. Talk about an ego boost. This setup was too convenient, though. There was no doubt they were hitting on her. "I feel like you're steering me away from some subjects. Like, how the two of you just happened to be here at the same time, talking to a woman you knew wouldn't pepper-spray you when you said you were gods."

"We were meeting down here regardless," Gwydion said. "I saw the stunning woman from this morning, and thought I'd say *hello*. Strictly coincidence, us meeting here."

She believed him. The parts he didn't gloss over, anyway. It bothered her a bit that she so easily trusted everything that came out of his mouth. That kind of naiveté got people killed. Or in her case, stripped of her rank, before being unwillingly saved from death.

The reminder clenched in her gut, calling back to a past she was here to pretend didn't exist. "What did you mean when you first walked up to me, by *this is usually where...*?"

Gwydion worked his jaw up and down. "Do you want the truth, which is completely unbelievable, or a lie that you won't accept because it's not the truth?"

"Surprise me." Kirby didn't know which would be worse, but apparently she wasn't going to buy his answer either way.

"Because you've lived more than a dozen lives before this one, and whenever we meet—you, me, Min—we always fall madly in love."

That was ridiculous. Completely ludicrous. Gods being real was one thing, but reincarnation was bullshit. If that were possible, the gods who ran TOM wouldn't be so terrified of death. "I bet you say that to all the girls you meet under bizarre circumstances."

"That depends on how you define *bizarre*," Min said dryly. He grasped her fingers, and heat rushed through her. "Nothing we say is going to convince you if you don't want to be swayed."

What he said was true. So why did his touch, his voice, and the sincerity in his gaze make her pulse race and her heart pound and her panties damp? Because part of her did believe him—both of them—and that was terrifying.

Then again, the fear was a little sweet, like marshmallows dipped in rock salt. She was down here to lose control and forget about the skeletons in her closet, and fucking two gods… That ranked pretty high on the *Ideas so Bad They're Good* list. "Let's push aside all the half-truths and back and forth for a minute, and admit this is about hooking up."

Both men nodded.

"Promise me"—she looked at Min; he was the one who filled her with the most delicious trepidation—"if I go up to your room, you can hurt me all you want, but you won't harm me."

Min cupped her cheeks between his palms and held her gaze. "I swear it, my huntress. I'll mark you. I'll own you. I'll make you scream with pleasure and pain. But I will never harm you."

This was ridiculous. Was she really going to swoon and fall in line, just because he repeated her words back at her? Yes. *Freya help me*, she trusted every word he'd said.

Starkad would blow a fuse if he found out she was being this kind of reckless. She was putting herself in danger. She was ignoring everything her training taught her, because two hot men were flirting with her, and she was horny and frustrated.

And Starkad had surrendered any right to an opinion on who she fucked or how.

CHAPTER THIRTEEN

5 YEARS AGO
KIRBY

Kirby felt like she was running through molasses. No matter how hard she pushed; her legs wouldn't go any faster. Invisible hands snatched at her naked body—grabbing, scratching, leaving heavy bruises and deep cuts.

Mark grabbed her arm, and a jolt of pain raced over her body. She tried to scream, but her voice was gone. Why couldn't she make a sound? Every inch of her hurt, as though she'd been stabbed in the gut. Burned until she couldn't breathe. Shot through the heart.

"My favorite toy." Mark flung her on her back and climbed on top of her.

She hit the ground hard, but the impact was just another tick on the *Everything Aches* list. Being flayed alive would bring her less pain.

Laughter rang in the air. Mark's. Brit's.

Knives that weren't there sliced her skin and peeled back the layers.

Kirby pleaded with herself to wake up. She didn't want to be here. She wanted this to stop.

Her eyes flew open, and she sat up with a start. Her heart hammered behind her ribs and her pulse throbbed in her skull. As the nightmare faded, her room swam into view. But it wasn't really *her* room. She was Starkad's guest. Had she screamed? If so, he'd be here soon, to check on her.

Part of her hoped he'd heard. He kept her sane after the dreams that haunted her every night. If he hadn't heard… she had alternatives. Pain. External distraction. That was tempting too. There was a high that came with the slice of razors on her skin. A rush that nothing else could compete with.

"Kirby." Starkad's voice drew her out of her thoughts. He stood in the doorway, watching her with concern. "Tell me what you need."

It was their shorthand. She could choose to talk about it or be distracted. She could choose to go back to sleep, but that was the last thing she wanted. Closing her eyes invited terror she couldn't fight. The one thing she couldn't pick was him. He hadn't held her since that first day, after he rescued her. Not that she expected him to, regardless of how much she wanted it.

"A distraction." Kirby forced the words out. Diving back into that fucked-up sludge of Freudian ubiquity was less appealing than… Actually, it sat so high on the *shitty* scale, she didn't have anything to compare it to.

He gestured toward the living room, and she followed.

They'd been here for almost a year, tucked away in a medium-sized suburb, hiding from TOM. For the first few months after Starkad saved her life, she tried to get him to explain why he'd done it. After enough vague answers and obvious changes of subject, she gave up.

She grabbed a controller off the shelf by the TV, flopped into the overstuffed chair she'd claimed as hers, and powered up the game system.

Starkad raised an eyebrow, but he mimicked her movements, settling into his own recliner. It didn't matter what game she loaded; he refused to play one on one against her. She wasn't great at The Hoarde, but he was worse.

So they played co-op. Shooting the heads off horde at fifty meters with a pulse rifle was the perfect way for her to forget her dreams. If she let him pick, he'd choose something like Monopoly or RISK, and he'd always win.

"Map or campaign?" she asked when the loading screen was up.

He selected his character. "You're letting me pick? Mighty generous of you. Campaign."

"What can I say? I'm a benevolent overlord." The light teasing was already chasing the shadows from her mind.

They stepped into the mission and immediately fell into their pace. He'd scout, she'd sneak. He ran into the room and drew fire. She stood in the darkness and picked off the baddies.

She still wondered why he'd given up everything for her. Not that she minded living with the literal object of some of her naughtiest fantasies, but that was her reason for appreciating the arrangement, not his.

The first few months they were here, he'd watched her closely. The longer she went without any incidents he was aware of, the more he eased off on the observation. As he gave her more freedom, he told her she could make her own choices. She could stay. She could go. But if she intentionally did anything that put either of them in danger, he'd walk away.

She didn't think he meant it, but she was terrified of finding out. There was only one rule of his she couldn't keep—the one where she was forbidden from hurting herself. The dreams consumed her most nights. People were wrong about one thing—when she died in her dreams, she always woke up after, wishing she hadn't.

If Starkad didn't hear her, sometimes she'd wake him up. Other times, the clawing need for something else overwhelmed her. She couldn't stay stuck in her own head, so she had to jar herself out. The razors tucked under her mattress were the solution. The first few times she'd done it, she wanted to find that same external pain she felt the night she almost died.

Then she'd discovered something new. With the right pain and mindset, there was a rush of euphoria that came after. A high she could lose herself in.

The crash sucked, but so did what came before the high, so she rode the buzz.

On screen, their exploding Jeep drew her full attention back to the game.

"*Bam.*" Starkad tossed his controller aside, and it landed on the coffee table with a clatter.

She grinned and shook her head. "It's thirteen grenades to fling us to the secret area."

"I used *thirteen grenades.*" His mocking tone was lightened by his smirk.

She never lost count. "You used fourteen."

He rolled his eyes. "Stupid Easter egg. It's just for a skull anyway."

"A skull that makes confetti explode out of people's heads." Kirby was kinder with her own controller as she set it aside. "I'm getting something to drink."

"Grab me one of whatever you're having?"

Kirby half-shrugged, half-nodded, and unfolded herself from her chair. She felt Starkad's gaze on her back, as she headed into the kitchen. The lightweight shorts and camisole she slept in were for comfort, but she didn't miss or mind the way he watched her when he thought she wasn't looking.

She grabbed two sodas from the fridge. Alcohol had never been a temptation. It churned in her stomach and made it harder to fight the demons. When she returned, she made a totally obvious display of bending at the waist, to set his drink on the table in front of him. Her reward was worth it. His gaze dropped below her neck, to where her top dipped low.

When he frowned, hurt slid in.

She straightened quickly, and turned away, heat burning up her neck. Stupid, stupid, stupid. She'd pushed too far. He didn't see her like that. Why did she dare think differently?

Starkad grabbed her wrist hard, drawing a gasp and yanked her to a stop.

Her pulse hammered in her ears. Was he interested, after all?

"Where did the cuts come from?" His soft question was heavy with disappointment.

Desire plummeted into humiliation. She jerked away and hugged herself. "What cuts? Nowhere. There are no cuts." She couldn't face him.

"Kirby. Look at me."

She couldn't ignore the command. As she turned, she studied her arms and how they crossed over her chest.

Starkad placed a finger under her chin and raised her head. Concern, not judgment, stared back at her from warm blue eyes. "Where did the cuts come from?"

A wave of lies rushed to the tip of her tongue, but none of them sounded legitimate. Even if she could come up with something realistic, she couldn't lie to him. "I… They distract me. When the memories are too much. When it hurts too much." Humiliation burned through her. He was going to kick her out now. Tell her she was worthless and weak, and force her to find her own way.

"We need to find you another way to cope."

We. She didn't know whether to laugh or sob at the word. "Like what?"

"Therapy. Talking to someone."

Damn him for sounding so kind about the whole thing.

"I can barely talk to you. And what am I supposed to tell a therapist? *A bunch of gods trained me to be a killer, and now I'm tortured because my girlfriend didn't love me after all?"* She pulled away from his touch.

"I can find you someone who will understand. And you don't need to trivialize it. This is hurting you. There are ways to make it stop."

"I found a way, thanks." She spun on her toe and stalked from the room. She couldn't do therapy. Telling someone what she'd been through? Reliving it, even through words? It was hard enough doing that in her sleep. Saying it aloud would rip her to shreds.

Besides, she could deal with trauma and pain. She was strong. She'd cope.

STARKAD

Starkad was lost. He didn't know how to help Kirby. She slept with her door locked now, and even when she did wake up screaming, she refused to let him in.

During the day, dark shadows hung under her eyes, and her skin was pale. That was if he saw her. For weeks after he discovered the marks on her skin, she went out of her way to avoid him.

He hated everything about this. What they'd done to her. Seeing her become a shell of his former student. Knowing this wasn't the Valkyrie he'd fallen in love with, but adoring this new, younger woman even more. And having her be just out of reach.

He had a solution, but he didn't dare suggest it. He'd done it a few times, before TOM, when Starkad was helping Gwydion deal with his demons. It was unconventional, and it was intense. But with her, it would hold a different meaning. He didn't know if he could ignore the temptation that would come with redefining her relationship with pain.

It had been almost a month since he confronted her, and she'd all but stopped eating. She spent most of her time hiding in her room.

The screams were louder tonight than they'd been since he and she first got here. And they didn't stop. Each time she cried out, it sliced straight to his heart.

Starkad couldn't sit back and do nothing anymore. He couldn't let her suffer alone. It only took a tight grip on the doorknob and a well-placed nudge with his shoulder, and he broke her lock. Charging into her room without permission was a forgivable sin, compared to finding a way to stop her pain.

Kirby stared at him, eyes wide, when he walked in. She was curled into a tiny ball. It took her a few seconds to focus on him.

He scooped her into his arms. Instead of fighting him, she gripped his shirt in her fists and leaned into him. He carried her back to his room, laid her on the bed, and wrapped himself around her.

She curled up against his chest with a whimper, her entire body shaking.

"I'm here. As much as you need." He whispered the comforts as much for himself as for her. He held her until her breathing evened and she drifted off to sleep, and didn't let go even then.

When she woke up several hours later, it was calmly, with the light flutter of eyelids and a few tiny, stunning sighs. She pressed into his chest, her skin scalding him through his shirt. "Why?" she asked softly.

"Because." He couldn't tell her more than that. *Gods*, he wanted to spill everything. Tell her the truth about where she'd come from. Stories of what they'd been together, once upon a time. This wasn't the time for any of that.

She forced herself to sit. "Okay."

"We have to deal with this somehow. This is destroying you."

Her laugh was strained. "I've already been destroyed. And I'm not letting anyone else inside my head. TOM was there for too long. They're still there."

"Doing nothing isn't an option. And what you're doing now isn't a solution. What are our next steps?"

"I don't know." She fiddled with the loose threads on his blanket.

Was he holding out because of fear for what it would do to her, or to him? She may not even be interested. She deserved to decide for herself. "I may have something to try. It stays between you and me. It doesn't require talking or diving into your head," he said.

"Sign me up." She met his gaze, hope in her eyes and voice.

"Don't agree before you know the details. You'll have full control, even when it feels like you don't. You say what your limits are. There's only one hard rule, and it's that this doesn't lead to sex." He had to be firm about that. He couldn't blur that line.

She licked her lips. "What kind of therapy has the potential to lead to sex?"

"Correction—there are two hard rules. Second is that you trust me." He needed to get on with the explanation. Would this tug on past life memories for her? Min had always liked his flogger, especially when Kirby was involved, and she enjoyed the play just as much.

"I do trust you." She said it so plainly and sincerely, the words made him ache. "What are we doing?"

"Teaching you new ways of accepting pain. Overcoming your negative associations. Learning that safety and security follow the hurting."

"That's both vague and a little too good to be true."

"Promise me first that you'll obey the rules. You don't have to commit to anything else until I explain, but I need your word now." Starkad wasn't an idiot. He could be oblivious at times, but it was hard to miss that she was as attracted to him as he was to her.

"I already promised the one." Hints of frustration were creeping in. "But all right. I swear I trust you and no sex."

If he dragged this out any more, talking about it would become insurmountable, rather than just the big deal he'd made it into. "Good. Your safeword is *defiance*."

Pink dotted her cheeks. "Safeword?"

"Don't forget it."

"Okay." Her irritation vanished in her breathy reply. "Defiance."

The concept was simple on the surface. He'd restrain her and administer pain. Bondage. Spanking. When he mentioned a cane, the way her chest heaved almost undid him.

Starkad walked her through everything. How she'd be restrained. The best way to keep her from being injured. He reminded her she had the power to say *stop* with her word. And checked in to make sure she was still okay with what he laid out.

He set a pillow near the edge of the mattress and told her to kneel. She complied without hesitation. The desire that thrummed through him carried memories of the past. Of being with Kirby in previous lives. He was rock hard, his cock threatening to strain his zipper. He pressed up against her back and inhaled softly. Under the soap and deodorant, he could smell fear and desire.

Fuck, that was tempting. "How are you doing?" he asked.

"Good." A tremor ran through her reply.

So delicious. He wrapped a silk scarf around his hand, then unwound it again. Each step was another closer to no return.

He wasn't kidding anyone. They'd passed that point long ago. He slipped the blindfold over her eyes, and her breath hitched.

When he tied it behind her head, her back went rigid.

"Kirby, talk to me," he said.

"I'm okay." She didn't sound so certain this time.

The trust had to flow both ways. If she said she was all right, he'd keep going. He slipped his finger along the elastic of her shorts and glided over her hip. The skin-on-skin contact was tantalizing. Her sigh was better.

He tugged and yanked her bottoms down in a single swift pull, exposing her ass.

Kirby whimpered. It sounded too much like the sound she made in her sleep. There was no excitement there. And then she sobbed.

No.

"Defiance." Her voice was so soft, he barely heard it.

He pulled the blindfold off as quickly as he could without hurting her. Her body quaked.

"I'm sorry." Her chin quivered, and her voice cracked.

He sank down next to her and pulled her into his lap. "It's okay," he murmured. "You never have to apologize for that."

But someone would pay for it. It might take years, or decades, but he'd exact a toll from Hel and Loki and everyone at TOM. And when he was done, he'd be the last person to atone. Until then, he'd make sure she was safe.

CHAPTER FOURTEEN

NOW
KIRBY

Fuck Starkad. Fuck what was smart or logical. Fuck her training. Because she was definitely fucking these gods. If her life ended tonight because of it, so be it. And if she survived the experience, she'd better have the time of her fucking life.

Kirby looked between Min and Gwydion. "Should we take this conversation someplace more… intimate?"

"Your wish is my desire, Huntress." Min grasped her fingers, kissed the back of her knuckles, and pulled her to her feet. He was a bit over the top, but it was alluring in its own way.

Why did he call her *Huntress?* Did he have any idea who she was? He couldn't. And she had decided not to care, so this was her, doing exactly that.

He led her to the elevator, and Gwydion joined them. Neither man touched her on the ride up. It was disconcerting, in a delicious *builds anticipation* sort of way. She was used to the guys she met pawing at her the instant she implied she'd sleep with them.

The opposite of Starkad. Whom these two were nothing like, because they'd actually acknowledged their interest in her.

But she wasn't caring about Starkad.

They rode to the top floor, where the hotel's two high-end suites were. If she was expected to be impressed by someone's money, she wasn't. Not that she'd complain about a little extra luxury.

Min unlocked the door and let them in. She had about two seconds to take in the expensive décor and vast room, before Gwydion cupped her face between his palms and crushed his mouth to hers.

She felt as though she'd been connected to a livewire, as showers of sparks raced through her veins. Intensity and frantic insanity bled through the connection. She gripped his shirt in her fists, holding on for all she was worth, and focused on every bit of his attention. She was learning to breathe again.

He followed a hungry path down her neck, then up, to nibble on her ear, before pressing his lips to hers again.

A new sensation joined the growing buffet. Min's breath caressed her cheek, and he pressed his chest into her back. "Do you have a safeword?" he asked.

"Defiance." Because how much more appropriate could that be right now, based on where she'd gotten it?

His chuckle rumbled through her. "I like that."

Gwydion's touch fell away, and a sharp spike of longing speared her. He brushed his lips over hers one more time, lightening the sting. "I'm going to watch for a little bit, if you're okay with that."

This entire thing flowed too smoothly. Min and Gwydion had done this before. They were gods. They'd probably had sex in every way imaginable, and some most people couldn't comprehend, thousands of times. As long as that meant they were good at it, Kirby didn't care. This was far from her first time joining a stranger in his hotel room.

Gwydion settled into a nearby chair, watching her. The electricity was back, sparking in her veins and dancing along her skin.

"Take off your dress." Min spoke like a man who wasn't used to hearing *no*. She liked that. "Leave the heels on."

Kirby couldn't fight her smile as she stripped the dress away and dropped it at her side. She looked good. Half a lifetime of a strict physical regimen meant her body was sculpted and sleek. And she didn't sport tan lines. Mostly because she liked to pretend it actually tormented Starkad when she sunbathed naked near the pool.

"You're not wearing much else," Min said with appreciation. He moved into view.

Her pulse was doing an interesting sort of tap-dance at the possessive desire in his gaze. "I didn't want many obstacles tonight." Was that too much information? He had said he preferred someone who knew how to play.

He hooked a finger in the elastic of her lacy underwear. The tiny patch of his skin brushing hers was white-hot. With a single tug, friction burned deliciously across her skin, and he tore the panties off.

Apparently that was possible.

Behind Min, Gwydion stroked the visible bulge inside his slacks.

"I like it." Min's voice was a low rumble.

She couldn't agree more.

Min grasped her arm. When his gaze fell to her wrists and the scars, a shard of humiliation disrupted her enjoyment.

"Who hurt you, Huntress?" He kissed the pale lines.

She struggled with the desire to jerk away. "I did. No one holds the power to hurt me, except me." She hoped that sounded as cold and powerful as she needed it to.

He gave a curt nod and looked her in the eye. "I understand."

Kirby doubted he did, but she was grateful he didn't push for more.

Min raised his hand to eyelevel and drew a tight circle in the air with his fingers. An invisible force gripped Kirby's wrists and trapped them above her head.

Magical bonds. Her heart pounded against her ribs. Since he put them there, it was likely only he could take them away. That added another flavor of fear to the parfait. Yummy.

She craved this feeling almost daily. The anticipation. Desire. Fear. She'd never found it this strong with anyone besides Starkad. There was a difference here, though. With Starkad, there had always been a sliver of knowledge—solid and practically tangible—that he wouldn't hurt her. Here, her heart thought she was safe, but her brain screamed at her to run. And there wasn't any pain yet.

Min stepped away, leaving her helpless, on display in the middle of the room. He rummaged through a suitcase and returned with two clamps on a chain.

Kirby's heart lodged in her throat. She raised her brows. "You travel with nipple clamps?"

"God of passion. I bring my work with me. Don't you?"

She did. But there was no way she was disclosing what that meant in her case. "Why not use magical ones?" She twisted her arms, to emphasize her point.

"There's something more primal about physical ones." He slapped her ass. "Careful with the talking back."

Kirby smirked. This was going to be fun. "Yes, sir."

Min wrapped the chain once around his hand, then glided both palms up her chest. His touch was soft, but the contrast between his skin and the cool metal was distinct. He teased her breasts with feather-light caresses—brushing his thumbs over her nipples, teasing the steel along her skin, lowering his head to suck and lick. He kept up the attention until she was panting and lightheaded.

When he pulled away, the cool air in the room kissed her damp skin. He set the clamps in place. The ache rocketed through her body, tugging at her core.

She squeezed her thighs together, hoping to sate the pulse. It didn't work.

"Are you enjoying yourself?" Min spanked her.

Her ass stung. "Yes."

"But you're terrified." He slapped the other cheek.

"Damn right, I am."

He glided his palm along the tender skin of her bare butt, both heating and soothing the pain. "If I ask you if you make a habit of this, will you tell me you're not normally that kind of girl?"

"If you spank me again, I'll tell you any lie you want to hear."

"Never. I never want you to lie to me."

She couldn't ignore the finality in his tone, but she could pretend he wasn't implying this would happen more than once. Whatever kind of role-play worked for him… "Would you prefer I begged? I'll do that."

"Hmm…" Min's deep growl rolled over her. He slipped a hand between her legs. She was so wet, the inside of her thighs were coated. "That's tempting." He teased her opening and slipped toward her clit. He stroked until she hovered on the edge of orgasm and was grinding into his hand, and then he pulled away.

Her pout was interrupted by a new zing of pain when he placed another clamp on her inner labia, below her swollen clit. That was new. It hurt like hell. She loved it.

The hold on her wrists vanished, and her arms fell to her sides, an ache spreading across her shoulders.

"Kneel," Min said.

She complied. This wasn't just about the high she got from the pain, though she was falling into that hard and fast. It was also about not being the one to think. Dropping her guard and letting herself be helpless. That wasn't an option in her everyday life, and doing it here was exhilarating.

"If you want me to stop, you can slap my leg." Min unzipped his slacks.

Kirby watched him with eyes that were probably as big as her expectations. She wasn't disappointed. She'd been with big guys before, but he was toeing that line of *novelty-sized.*

He gripped her hair hard enough to yank her scalp, and shoved his cock in her mouth. Tears welled in her eyes when he hit the back of her throat. She choked through her gag and relaxed enough to let him in.

With her hands free, she could reach up with one, to stroke his sac. The clamps had become a dull, persistent ache. Enough to remind her of their presence. She slipped her other hand between her legs. Toward the need that pulsed there.

"I didn't say you could do that." Warning edged Min's words.

She planted her palm on her thigh instead, to steady herself.

He fucked her face without reserve, his groans becoming grunts as his thrusts grew shorter. His balls tightened under her touch. He shuddered when he came, spilling in her mouth, a hint dribbling down her chin.

Kirby dragged her tongue along his shaft as he slid from her mouth.

Min knelt in front of her. He ran his thumb over her chin, smearing his cum, and kissed her softly. "How are you doing?"

Did her tongue still work? "Horny," she managed.

Gwydion laughed. She'd almost forgotten he was here.

Min scooped her into his arms. This felt familiar. And right. He laid her on her back on the bed, and the invisible restraints returned to bind her arms above her head.

He pulled the clamps from her nipples. Sharp needles tingled under her skin, as the blood rushed back. It was hot and cold and delicious. He kissed each tender nub softly, amplifying the sensation of feeling returning to the area.

The mattress shifted when Gwydion knelt between her legs. "I'm done watching."

The pressure vanished from her clit as well, and the feeling in her breasts was mimicked between her thighs. Then two pairs of mouths were on her, sucking and licking. Teasing her body as it woke up.

When Gwydion slid two fingers inside her and hooked them up, to press her G-spot, that déjà vu feeling returned. The way he coaxed her yanked her thoughts back to him. He wrapped his lips around her clit and fingered her.

She was so close to orgasm, she came quickly, bucking against his face and clenching around him.

Min's touch on her nipples stayed consistent—light, playful, and enhancing the lingering sting.

Gwydion nudged her opening with the head of his cock and slid inside without further warning. He stretched her out and drew a moan. Fuck, that felt good.

He glided in and out slowly at first. As he picked up the pace, he returned to tease her clit. She hovered right on the edge between his touch feeling incredible and it being too much.

Another climax crawled through her with deliciously slow torment. Hinting that she was almost there. Mocking her with the agony of anticipation. Pleasure crashed around her, and she screamed at the release.

That seemed to unleash Gwydion. He pounded inside her frantically, drawing out her orgasm. She lost herself in the maze of every pleasure center firing in her brain at the same time.

He grunted, and she swore she felt him spill in her. As he slowed then stopped, he stayed buried inside her.

Kirby slipped away from the edge of ecstasy, but the feeling didn't vanish completely.

Gwydion leaned in for a hungry kiss. Another of those that obliterated any reason she might have.

He finally slipped out of her. Min pulled her back into him, and Gwydion lay across from her. He pressed his forehead to her breastbone, then peppered her with a smattering of tiny kisses, before he settled in.

A fuzzy thought flitted in the back of her mind. The only time she'd ever felt this safe was when Starkad used to hold her.

The notion carried a hint of bitterness, and she shoved it aside in favor of living in the now.

Chapter Fifteen

5 Years Ago
Starkad

After the aborted attempt with the spanking, Kirby fell asleep next to Starkad.

He was grateful to see her sleep through the night, but the next morning, she was withdrawn. Refusing to make eye contact. Speaking in single-word replies, even when he assured her there was nothing wrong with her reaction.

She claimed exhaustion at about seven that night, and vanished into her room.

Starkad didn't argue. He did settle in on the couch with a book, and one ear turned in her direction.

After centuries of living in warzones and worse, sleep was more of a luxury for him than a necessity. He didn't have an issue with holding vigil all night, to ensure she was all right. He'd done it before, and he suspected he'd do it hundreds of times again.

A few hours passed without incident. Then the sound of a door opening caught his attention.

He looked up as Kirby padded into the living room. She stopped about a meter back, gaze turned to her feet, and tugged down the hem of a T-shirt that wasn't quite long enough to hide her panties.

The shy, demure posture would have been electrifying, if it weren't so out of character.

He waited, not wanting to say anything to derail the conversation before it started.

"I want to try again." Her voice was so soft, he could have imagined the words.

Desire coursed through him, bringing his senses to life. "Okay."

"But maybe not so scary? Is that an option?" She finally looked up.

The contrast of this trained assassin looking vulnerable and uncertain was startling. And he almost hated himself that it made him instantly hard. "It is. Anything you need this to be, we'll figure out how to make it work. Come here." He added a hint of command to the latter words.

When she drew within reach, he grabbed her wrist. She tensed as he jerked, tugging her to lie over his knees. She relaxed when her body met his. Her warm weight pressed into him, and his dick strained to get closer.

He ignored his own need. If there was one thing the last millennium had taught him, it was patience. He drew his fingers lightly up the back of her bare legs.

She squirmed and gasped.

Fuck, that was enticing.

He lifted her shirt, grabbed the elastic of her panties, and tugged up, wedging them in place and exposing her ass. When he slapped the bare skin, the *crack* echoed through the room.

She groaned and relaxed further into his legs. "Besides feeling good, how is this supposed to help, again?"

"The pleasure is part of the point." Hers and his. He spanked her again. A faint pink spread across each ass cheek. "There are no extra consequences here." *Slap.* "There's only now." *Slap.* "And you're in control of how and when." *Slap.*

"So I can say *don't stop*, and you'll keep going?"

A groan rose in his chest, and he swallowed it. "As long as it's safe."

"Don't stop." Her request was an intoxicating blend of timid and insistent.

Odin, he was so screwed. Starkad alternated between cheeks. Each time his palm made impact with her skin, she rubbed against him and made a delicious new sound.

Her giggles faded into muted moans. She was slipping into that space where the endorphins took over.

Her butt almost glowed red, and her sighs were soft and distant.

"That's enough," he said, half-expecting an argument. He ran a soothing touch over her tender flesh. It would be so easy to lean in and kiss away the sting. To glide his fingers between her legs—

"Okay." Her reply was barely a whisper.

He helped her sit on the cushion next to him. "Do you need anything? Water?"

"No. I'm good here." She curled her legs under her and leaned her head against his shoulder. "I can stay here for a while, can't I?"

"Always."

As Kirby drifted into sleep, she shifted to lay her head on his leg. This was both better and worse than the spanking. She was right here. Finally in his arms. Close. Comfortable. Enticing.

And she was still so far out of his reach.

He didn't know he'd drifted off until he awoke to the clatter of dishes. He was alone on the couch. That explained the smell of coffee that greeted him. He scrubbed some of the sleep from his face and wandered into the kitchen.

Kirby stood by the stove, fully clothed, making scrambled eggs. "Good morning." Her wet hair hung loose down her back, leaving damp spots on her T-shirt. She wore a soft smile.

It had been lifetimes since he saw her look like this. Any doubt he had about last night evaporated. "Morning. There enough of that for me to have some?"

"I didn't want yours to get cold before you woke up." She slid the eggs onto a plate that already had bacon, and held it out. "But you can take this one. I'll make more."

He was getting full sentences out of her and everything. "No, but thank you." He shook his head. "I'm going to shower." Because he didn't know if he was still hard from last night, or hard again from seeing Kirby content, but he needed some privacy to alleviate the pressure.

A frown whispered across her face.

"Eat while it's hot," Starkad said. "And make sure mine is ready in thirty minutes."

"Yes, sir." Her smile was back, more hesitant but still reaching her eyes.

This felt dangerous. A nagging voice in the back of his head said he was lying to himself about what was happening. As long as Kirby was safe—not waking up screaming in the middle of the night and not cutting herself—he was willing to swim in denial.

He locked his bedroom door and shed his clothes as he headed into the bathroom. His semi-erect cock sprung free.

He stepped into the shower, letting too hot water sear over him. It didn't burn away the need slicing through his veins. There was no way to ignore the potent memories of last night. Kirby's weight against his legs. Her smooth ass growing pinker with each slap. Those delicious little groans and sighs she made.

Starkad fisted his shaft hard and stroked. More images flooded his thoughts. Of their first life together. The two of them, naked on blankets of fur. His glorious Valkyrie, riding him, the firelight glistening on her pale skin.

His thoughts—his body—weren't satisfied to linger in the past. Fantasies joined the mix. Of Kirby surrendering herself. Yielding to his touch. The hint of vanilla from her body-wash teasing his senses.

Him, stripping her down a piece of clothing at a time. Taking his time devouring her body. Sliding inside her tight, slick pussy.

He came hard, coating his hand, cum washing away in the shower and spiraling down the drain. He didn't stop stroking until his dick was sore and protesting. The images continued to torment him, though.

As days turned into weeks then months, the nights Kirby woke up terrified grew less frequent, and she was more outgoing during the day. Spanking turned into a hairbrush, his belt, a wooden spoon… It depended on how playful either of them felt.

She never stopped trying to hide the scars on her wrists, though. She preferred long-sleeved shirts, and kept her hands tucked away when that wasn't an option.

He had a solution for that, too. Her face lit up when he gave her the small box wrapped in plain blue paper. "What is it?" she asked.

"Open it and find out."

She tore the wrapping off, bottom lip caught between her teeth, and smile teasing the corners of her mouth. "Oh." The delighted gasp escaped when she opened the box. "For me?"

"Happy… anniversary?" That carried all sorts of assumptions, but it was true. He'd pulled her out of TOM a year ago.

The twist of her lips implied she didn't care for the term either. "Birthday? Technically, I was reborn that day."

"All right. Happy birthday."

She pulled one decorative leather bracer out. "Help me put them on?"

"Hold out your arms." He buckled one into place, and then the other.

KIRBY

Kirby rolled her arms, examining the new accessories. They made a bold statement, and they covered the scars. Giddiness sparked inside. Starkad was so good to her. She still didn't know why, but she was grateful.

"I love them. Thank you." She threw her arms around his neck in a tight hug.

He squeezed back, and she let his warmth flow through her. It was harder than she'd thought possible, to not beg him to fuck her after their sessions. Every inch of her craved his touch. But as long as she could have some sort of contact, she was content.

She stepped back, studying the gifts. They weren't practical for anything she'd been trained to do. They were completely decorative, and didn't really compliment the jeans and T-shirts she preferred. But she loved them regardless.

She traced her finger over the polished steel loop on one. "What are these for?" Anticipation sped through her, nudging her senses with possibility, but she couldn't put a name to her desire.

"They're an assumption. I hope you don't mind."

"What do they assume?"

He grasped her fingers and led her to his bedroom.

Desire thrummed under her skin. Any kind of assumption that landed her here was enough to make her pulse hammer in her ears.

He guided her to the side of the bed. A bar hung from the ceiling. That was new. A latch was attached to each end.

"You wanted to take things to a new level." His deep voice rolled over her. He grasped one of her wrists and attached it to the bar, and then the other.

It left her arms above her head, and her restrained and helpless. Holy fuck, could he hear how hard her heart hammered against her ribs?

"Are you good?" he asked.

"Yes." She managed through her suddenly dry throat. Nods weren't allowed when he checked in with her. She had to say the words. In the past, he'd cuffed her. They'd gone back to the blindfold on occasion.

But this was a new level of intense. The promise of what came next was enough to make her panties damp.

He moved behind her. "Do you want to try something new?" the heat of his throaty question caressed her neck.

"Gods, yes."

At Starkad's low chuckle, a whimper slipped out without her permission. He glided a thumb under her waistband, starting at her hip and moving forward, then undid her jeans. He pushed those and her panties to her knees, leaving her exposed and restrained twice over.

The contact stopped. There was always a pause. He did a delicious job of making her wait. Sometimes it was seconds. Other times, longer. She was never disappointed with the results.

The sharp whistle of something narrow slicing the air teased her. She clenched her jaw, eager and waiting.

A deep sting raced through her when the cane struck the fleshiest part of her ass, and she cried out in surprise and pain. Holy hell, she liked that feeling.

There was a pause, and then another strike. The crack flooded her veins with endorphins, a delicious high of terror and pleasure.

She lost count after a couple of strikes, happy to slide into her own head. She trusted Starkad to stop when needed, and if she asked sooner, he'd comply.

When the caning finished, the buzz lingered, stealing her thoughts and letting her float on a cloud. She was only half-aware of Starkad unhooking her from the bar, and making sure she kept her balance while she stepped out of her jeans.

"Lie on the bed, on your stomach." His voice was kind but firm.

She complied without question. The ache was sinking in as the buzz faded. She wouldn't be sitting much for the next few days, and it would be a couple of weeks before they did something this intense again.

Kirby was okay with that.

Wasn't she?

Reality crawled back into her thoughts, bringing the past with it. What was she doing? Playing a silly game with a man who was… She didn't even know. Doubt clawed under her skin and dragged her toward a gaping pit.

This was stupid. She was stupid. How long did she think this could last? Why couldn't she deal with her demons on her own?

"*Kirby*." Starkad draped a towel over her butt, and the soft terrycloth bit into the fresh marks. A cool weight rested on top of it all. That would be the ice. He lay next to her, on his side. "Hey," he said softly, drawing her gaze. "Stay here with me." He brushed a strand of hair behind her ear.

She nodded and focused on his voice. His touch. His kindness.

The ritual continued through one *birthday*, and then another. As time bled away, it was easier for Kirby to shove her past into a box at the back of her mind.

Starkad would leave sometimes, for days or even a week. He said it had to do with his time at TOM. He was vague on details, telling her he wanted her as far from that life as possible.

Kirby felt her sanity slipping every time she lingered in her memories for too long, so she didn't push for more.

It was easy to pretend they had a normal life. That the playing house they did was real. Especially when they went out, and drew both admiring and envious stares and whispers, she could mostly convince herself they were a couple.

Until her mind screamed back with the reminder they weren't. There were a few things missing. The verbal commitment. Transparency. Honesty. And the fact that she wanted more—her body craved it—from their sessions.

She couldn't be the only one. She'd see how hard he got. Knew that he was jerking off in the shower the morning after.

As he unhooked her cuffs from the bar one evening, the desire thrumming in her was more intense than ever. Moisture coated the insides of her thighs, and her body pleaded to take this moment to the next level.

When he told her to get comfortable on the bed, she turned to him instead and grasped his wrist.

"Kirby?" Warning cut through his question.

"Fuck me. Please?" She drew his fingers between her legs, to stroke along her slit. "I know I'm not the only one who wants it."

"No." He yanked away and stepped back.

Humiliation burned inside, hot and violent. "You said I could ask for whatever I needed." This childish retort slipped out.

"I said no sex. You promised me." There was an edge to his tone.

She couldn't be the only one who wanted more to happen between them. Pride insisted she push this until she got the answer she wanted. The one that was real. "That was more than two years ago. How are you ignoring this… this intense, white-hot aura that surrounds and engulfs us? How do you not care?"

He clenched his jaw. She'd pushed too hard. But she couldn't keep walking this line.

"If I didn't care, you wouldn't be here." Starkad's emotion vanished behind a blank mask.

"Then maybe I'm sorry you care." She ignored his glare, gathered her clothes, and stalked from the room.

Walking away didn't soothe her humiliation at the rejection, but it did kill the horniness. She locked her bedroom door behind her and collapsed on her stomach on her bed.

Her mind was numb. Her ass was sore. She was an idiot. She'd done it again. Just like with Brit. Misinterpreted what was there.

At least Starkad hadn't sold her out to the gods at TOM as vengeance. Maybe that was still coming, but she didn't think so. Not after all they'd been through.

Her bracer chafed her wrists. Another reminder of how gullible she was. She fumbled with the buckles until she managed to yank them off, then threw them across the room. They slapped into the closet door and fell harmlessly to the carpet.

She wouldn't let this become what it had with Brit, where Kirby made assumptions, and paid the price because of it. Resolution churned inside. For years, she'd been climbing out of the darkness, and she refused to tumble back in.

She showered, washing away the shame and desire, and steering clear of the marks on her backside. After she was dry, she tugged on a loose dress, grabbed the bracelets from the carpet, and steeled herself.

Starkad was in the living room, doing a poor imitation of reading.

"I'm sorry." She winced at how weak the apology sounded.

He looked up, eyebrow raised. A frown flitted across his face when his gaze fell on her hands.

She crossed the room and set the bracers on the coffee table.

"These were a gift," he said.

"And I appreciate them. And what they stood for." She reached past all the doubt, to grab the steel that had kept her sane when she was with TOM. "But it's time for me to move past that with you."

"Ruby—"

"Let me finish." She didn't remember when she'd started noticing the nickname, but hearing it now sliced through fresh wounds. "I've been a drain on you for years. You've done a lot for me, and I haven't done anything in return." *Freya*, this *being mature* stuff sucked. She didn't want to be doing this. She wanted to whimper and beg and plead for things to go back to what they had been. To curl up on his lap and be comforted.

But that was dangerous to her sanity.

"You don't need to do anything."

"I do need to." Her voice cracked. "Tell me where you go. What you do. It has to do with taking down TOM, doesn't it? Tell me what I need to know, to help."

Starkad set his book on the coffee table, next to her discarded bracers, and studied her. "You're out. You never have to go back in."

"I'm not out. I can stuff my past aside and pretend it's not there, but it is. And I can't be a drain on you for the rest of my life. Please." As Kirby spoke, she realized how desperate she was to be more. To do more. "Tell me what you're doing and how I can be a part of it."

Starkad sighed, and silence stretched between them. She resisted the urge to count the seconds.

"They're called the Followers of Urd," he finally said.

Chapter Sixteen

Now - Kirby

Kirby wasn't embarrassed by what she'd done. Last night was incredible. Her reckless actions should have landed her somewhere other than eight hours of heaven.

And then someone woke them up this morning, hammering on the hotel room door. She sat up in bed, wrapped in sheets and still pressed against Gwydion, while Min answered. It was Starkad.

There was a twinge in her chest that she couldn't identify, as all three men stared each other down. There was also a question she very much understood. How did Starkad know which room she was in?

"Is this man a problem?" Min asked.

In so many ways. "He's a colleague." Mentor. Friend. Savior. Not-lover. And he had no right to judge her.

Not that he was.

She refused to be demure or shy now. She let the sheet drop away and tugged on her dress, intently aware of the three pairs of eyes on her. Heat filled her, amplified by the friction of fabric on her skin. She swore the tension and desire in the room flowed together in an almost tangible fog.

She approached Min. He caught the base of her neck and pulled her into him, to claim her mouth. Her body molded to his. She groaned at the power and intensity in his kiss.

Before he pulled away, he murmured against her lips, "Thank you for an incredible night, Huntress."

"Ooh, me too." Gwydion grabbed her wrist and spun her. He laid a series of playful nibbles along her bottom lip before kissing her hard. The way he danced his fingers along her hips, and inched up the hem of her skirt, made her giggle, but his hard body drew a groan.

He kissed along her jaw, to nip her earlobe. "Until next time," he whispered, then tugged his cap back onto her head.

There wouldn't be a next time. The thought hurt more than should be possible, especially since she didn't know him and Min. So she smiled. She was keeping the hat, though.

Starkad cleared his throat with an exaggerated cough. "Are we all having fun?"

She rolled her eyes and turned to face him. He wasn't looking at her.

Jealous bastard. What gave him the right? "Let's go." She brushed past him without a second glance.

She stalked back to the elevator, and he kept pace. The ride down to their floor was spent in awkward silence.

"My room." He clipped off the words.

She clenched her jaw. She wanted to shower. Put on different clothes. Spend a little longer ignoring him. But last night had cleared most of the self-destructive out of her system, and she needed to be a professional, not a brat.

Really, what gave him the fucking right to be pissed about this? And she still wanted to know how he found her. Questions that could wait until they were behind closed doors.

He unlocked the door, and they stepped inside. He stalked across the room, grabbed a box off the table, and tossed it at her. "You're going to be a brunette."

She caught the dye easily and set it on the dresser next to her. "I read online that brunettes are kinkier. Do you think that's true?"

"And you get your wish. Your target is still here, so we are too." He never looked at her, and his voice was like ice, sliding down her spine.

"Yay. Hurray." Despite the lack of enthusiasm in her words, adrenaline spilled inside, mixing anticipation with anxiety. Brit was here. There would be vengeance.

Starkad whirled on her, eyes narrowed. "What's your malfunction?"

"Me?" Kirby scoffed. "You're one to talk, ice man."

"You're supposed to be keeping a low profile. Not fucking random strangers you met in a bar."

Her irritation surged. "Hi. Have you met me? Do you have any idea how I spend my free time? I've never made a secret of it."

"You were in his room."

"Which… how did you know where to find me?"

Starkad's gaze flicked away from her for the briefest second. "The bartender saw who you left with." He was lying. Fuck him.

"Would you rather we'd gone back to my room?" she asked. "This isn't the first time I've done it, and it certainly won't be the last."

He gripped the back of the chair next to him so hard, the wood creaked. "I need you to take this more seriously. That's not a random TOM out there. It's Brit. She's—"

As good as I am when she doesn't hold back. That was the last thing Kirby wanted to hear. The truth sucked like that. "She's what?" She put an edge in her voice.

"Be. More. Careful. This situation is different."

"No it's not. This is exactly the same as every other time I've hooked up while we're on mission. Cautious is second nature for me. It's been drilled into my skull for as long as I can remember. I was trying to be careless last night, and I was still safer than ninety-nine percent of the world."

"You were trying…?" He raised his brows.

Oh fuck him and his judgment. "Why are you so upset about this specific instance?"

"That one percent is Brit. And if she finds you first…" He just had to throw that in her face.

"What am I supposed to do instead? Stay locked in my room and be celibate? Because you're sure not going to fuck me." Never mind that she was the one who wanted to stay yesterday. This was about every time.

"This isn't about you and me." Another lie. Asshole.

"But it is, isn't it? Because you're lying to me. You're acting jealous." As Kirby said the word, she realized how true it was. It was hard to believe. He'd pushed her away for years. But her training, her instinct—everything said this attitude was different from what it had been in the past.

Starkad was jealous.

And she was smug.

Starkad's roar shook her to her core. He whirled on her and stalked forward until her back was to the wall. "I do this to keep you safe. I don't care for resentment in return. You don't want from me what you're asking for."

Sex? She did. She had for years. Her pulse hammered in her ears. "I've told you that's exactly what I want. *You're* exactly what I want. You want me to stop screwing around? Give me an alternative."

"I would do so much for you, but that's not an option."

With him this close, she could drown in everything about him. His strength. His heat. His cool, familiar scent.

"Then you have no right to be jealous if I find it somewhere else. I've never made a secret of whose bed I'd rather be in." She squirmed against him, not to get away, but to feel more. Satisfaction wormed inside when his hard length pressed into her hip. "To quote Cheap Trick, I want you to want me."

"No. You don't."

Kirby searched his face. What she saw hints of caught her off guard. "What are you afraid of?"

"Things you can't begin to comprehend. But not that."

"Bullshit. Why does the idea of fucking me scare you? You hide your fear well, but it's there. It trickles from you." Though some of that was her. Need screamed in her veins and hammered in her thoughts, mingling with the delicious terror of what would happen if she pushed him too hard.

"Fine. You think this is really what you want?" He spoke through clenched teeth.

Even pinned between him and the wall, she had a little wiggle room. She stood on her tiptoes and crushed her mouth to his. The kiss sparked over her skin. So this was what it was like to taste him. She could fall into the sensation, but not yet. Not under these circumstances. She bit his lip hard when she pulled away.

Starkad snarled and pressed his hand to her in throat, locking her in place. The weight on her windpipe was just enough to fuzz her thoughts, and it was incredible. She welcomed the pain, but the unleashed lust that raged behind his gaze terrified her.

He kissed her hard enough to cut her lips into her teeth. His hungry, furious kiss stole her thoughts. He returned the favor of the bite several times over, until her lips were swollen and tender, and her body whimpered for more.

STARKAD

Starkad had held back for years. Watching Kirby. After she was an adult, wanting her. Telling himself he had to wait because making their relationship sexual wasn't appropriate. It was all a series of excuses. He'd crossed the point of no return with Kirby long ago. The first time he landed his palm against her bare ass. Or was it when he suggested the play in the first place?

Was it before then?

This morning, he'd assumed she was in her room. He was looking for Min, not her, to confirm Gwydion was here too. And because he'd hoped Min would be a voice of reason.

When Starkad saw her with them… Kirby was partly right; there was jealousy. Mostly though, it was desire. When he'd promised himself he wouldn't love her in this life, he had no idea how much that pushed the limits of his self-control.

He wanted her. He needed her. And he desperately loved her. Possibly more than he had in her first life.

And now she stood trapped between him and the wall, reeking of sex. He didn't care that it was because of how she spent her night. She pushed all his buttons this morning, and snapped his control.

Starkad grabbed her arm and yanked her into him. Her delighted gasp was fuel, poured on the flames licking over his skin. He spun her away, hoping the action would quench his desire when he wasn't looking her in the eye.

She pressed back into him, grinding her ass into his erection.

Fuck it all. He pushed her toward the bed, and she knelt without protest. He flipped up her skirt to reveal her bare ass, her pussy teasing him from between her legs.

Starkad's reason was gone. He grabbed her wrist, tugged it behind her back, and pressed her face first into the mattress, leaving her behind up the in the air.

Kirby could twist out of this. She knew a dozen rolls, and a couple would probably catch him off-guard. She also knew the one word that would make him stop.

Instead, she groaned and wiggled her hips.

His heart hammered against his ribs, and his pulse screamed. When he unzipped his pants, she whimpered. If he weren't already unraveled, that would have been the final straw.

He thrust inside her without warning, burying himself deep. She was tight, and slick with need, squeezing his cock. This angle would strain her shoulder and steal her balance. Leave her with just enough of an ache to remember the moment.

They both preferred it that way.

Starkad reached around to tease her clit. There was no time or patience for tenderness and buildup. He needed her to come. He needed so much from this moment.

He stroked her swollen button hard, barely moving inside her. Her climax swept up quickly. She clenched around him and bucked away from his touch. He didn't ease up until she shuddered with pleasure.

A tiny bit of him wanted her to be the voice of reason. To stop this.

But he was grateful she didn't. He moved both his hands to grip her hips, and slammed inside her. He was lost in the coppery tinge of control and power that clouded his thoughts whenever he took Kirby. He pounded hard, hitting her at the right angle inside. Letting the friction build. Listening to her cues.

He struggled to hold back, but when she came a second time, he couldn't. Spikes danced through his nerves. His balls were tight. Stars sparked behind his eyelids.

The world paused for a heartbeat, and climax spilled from him, into her. He fucked her until the edge dulled and reality licked the corners of his vision.

Starkad slid out of her and let her go. He enjoyed the sex, but he didn't like losing control.

Kirby rolled onto her back, a playful smile playing on her face. She stretched her shoulders and rolled her neck. "So worth the wait." Her voice was soft. She was stunning. Glowing. Half-naked.

"Happy now?" His growl was weak. He'd lost his grip on the reins. With the one person he swore he never would.

"Yes, sir," she said demurely.

He knelt next to her and cradled her face between his hands. He brushed his lips lightly over hers. The spark that raced through him almost stole his reason again. It had been so long, and this felt so right.

Starkad always held her after sessions. This was different. He needed it more than ever, and suspected she did too. He dragged a thumb over her cheek, studying her eyes. The woman who stared back devoured his breath and filled his heart with warmth.

"I didn't want this. Not this way." The regret slipped out without his permission.

She went rigid against his touch.

Fuck. *Fuck fuck fuck.*

Kirby jerked away and stood. "Fuck you." She kept her back to him as she smoothed out her dress. She strode toward the door.

"Kirby, don't you dare—" But he couldn't put the power in his command. He'd just changed their entire relationship.

She paused with her hand on the doorknob, her body straight as a rod. When she turned to him, her face was a stony mask. He'd seen this expression on mission, but never outside of it.

"All right. I'll stay." Her voice was cool. "We don't even have to talk about what happened. I'd hate to think I was a regret for you, in any way."

"That's not—"

"You said we'd pursue Brit. That means she's in town still?"

"Yes." Starkad racked his brain for the right words to explain.

"Great. I need a shower. Maybe you'll like me more as a brunette. Actually, who gives a shit what you like? I'll talk to you when I get out."

He let her walk out of the room. He needed to cool down, and so did she. This was on him, and he wanted her to heal, not regressing into what she'd been when he pulled her out of TOM.

A shower sounded like a good idea. Her scent clung to everything, clogging his nostrils and thoughts.

His phone chimed, and he grabbed for it.

Brit.

"Yeah?" he said.

"I want out. Asylum."

Starkad didn't have the time or patience for this. He wasn't some revolving door for TOMs who decided they were fed up with the lifestyle. "Good luck with that."

"Wrong answer. I've fed you information for years. I've put everything on the line. I want something in return." Her voice was tight.

Had this been her plan with this trip? Surprise him by being the team leader, then ask for his help walking away? "You get salvation. Helping me is atonement for your guilt." A sliver of guilt wormed its way through him. Seeing what Kirby had gone through over the last few years made him rethink ever being involved with TOM, even as a double agent. Now he had the chance to save someone else.

The person who almost cost him everything.

"Yeah. Atonement. For the death of a woman who's not dead after all. And you knew it. Why didn't you tell me Kirby was alive?"

Because that was the last thing he needed—Brit, hounding him for contact with Kirby, so… What? So she could destroy Kirby a second time? The first round was rough enough. "Are you actually asking me why?" he asked.

"You pulled her out. Do the same for me. You don't have to take me under your wing. Give me a name. A connection. Something." Desperation leaked into her plea. "You have people who relocate target survivors. Put me in touch with that group."

"You've made contacts. Call one of them."

"TOM contacts. I seriously don't have time to argue with you. Mark will wonder why I'm taking secret phone calls."

"Then accept my *no* and hang up." Starkad didn't know why he was still on the line. "If I help you get out, Kirby will know where you are. Do you want to survive retirement?"

"Are you fucking her?"

The question wouldn't have meant anything yesterday. Or an hour ago. Now it made him want to put his fist through the wall. "She's my ward and my student." Not that he owed Brit any explanation.

"She's a grown woman who adored you. Did you ever even see that? Not sure how you could miss it. When she wasn't busy ignoring the impact she had on my life, she was lusting after you. She would have given everything to bow at your feet."

Starkad hated the truth in those words. Not because of the idea, but because he was the one who kept it from happening. "This conversation is over."

"Wait," Brit half-shouted. "Please? This isn't about her. *Vidar*, it's a relief to know she's still alive. And I just want out."

His answer should be *no*. If anyone else had helped him the way Brit had, he'd consider their request. "I'll see what I can do. I'll be in touch." He disconnected.

This entire situation was a problem. Kirby wanted vengeance, he almost believed Brit was sincere about wanting to walk away from TOM, and there was no question which of them Starkad's loyalties lay with.

For all he knew, Brit's help over the years had been a way for her to feed him the names of anyone she deemed as a threat to her position. Similar to what she'd done to Kirby—let someone else pull the trigger on the obstacle.

He had another concern, too. If he helped hunt Brit, it could destroy Kirby in ways she might never come back from.

One thought stood out clearly, amid the uncertainty. He'd kill Brit without hesitation before she could touch Kirby.

Chapter Seventeen

Now
Brit

Brit could handle pain. She had the techniques down, to ignore it long enough to accomplish critical tasks. Mark had played a huge part in that.

Right now, she wasn't in the mood to block out one more thing. Her shoulder throbbed, her ear hurt like a bastard, and Starkad wasn't yielding.

"Well?" Mark watched her expectantly.

"He told me he'd think about it. But I'm not worried. He'll cave."

"How do you know?"

Brit didn't. For all she knew, Starkad would either ignore her or tell her to go fuck herself. She kept her doubt tucked deep down. "Because he won't want to break Kirby." She wasn't sure how she knew that, but a guy who gave up his entire life to rescue a single girl had to have some attachment to her. And Starkad had infuriated gods when he walked away from TOM.

Brit hated playing both sides of this fence. She wouldn't turn on Starkad. She'd still kill Mark the instant she had her out. But letting Mark think otherwise was safest. If he believed he was in on everything she was doing, he'd spend half as much time poking around behind her back, trying to figure out what she was up to. She wasn't in any condition to fend him off if things went bad.

"What have you helped him with?" Mark asked.

She had this answer. She'd come up with it before she even placed the call to Starkad. "I fed him bullshit training intel. Stuff that checked out but doesn't matter in the long run." She'd figured out details too, if Mark needed them. No reason to offer more information than he asked for. The best lies were the simplest and bore some resemblance to the truth.

"And you never realized he'd been working you the same way you've been working him." Mark chuckled.

Brit lay back on her bed, letting exhaustion creep in. "Working me how?"

"Never telling you Kirby was alive. Do you really think they're fucking?"

She was really trying not to think about it. She meant every word on the phone, but that didn't mean she wanted the image in her head of her ex-girlfriend riding their former combat instructor. "If Kirby wanted him, she got him. We both know she doesn't give up."

"Fair enough." He settled next to her, a few inches between them. "What do you want to do until he gets back to you?"

Brit should be grateful he was dropping the subject so quickly. She'd known Mark so long that it sent suspicion coursing through her instead. "Sleep until things don't hurt so much."

"I'll leave you to that. Do you want to get cake later?" He sounded nice. Not just polite, but like he actually cared. When he was this kind, he wanted something, but what?

"Are you making a grocery store run or something?" she asked.

He shrugged. "I could. Or there's a local place that's open late. I guess they're like a bakery night club? No idea how that works. We could have Irish coffee and German chocolate cake."

"What are you up to?" She was too tired to second- or third-guess Mark's mind games.

"Why do I have to be up to anything?"

She squeezed her eyes shut and scrubbed her face. "Because you're being nice. As in, nice-guy nice. As in, manipulative-asshole nice."

He rolled his eyes. "We're partners. This Kirby shit has to be messing with your head. You're injured, and I'm worried about you."

"Cake sounds good." Brit didn't buy that his concern was genuine, but she wasn't surprised that he sounded sincere. He'd always excelled at that.

So they'd go get cake, and she'd try to hide how impatient she was for Starkad to call her. To tell her he had her back. She needed a contingency plan, in case he told her *no*. No one hid from TOM, but Kirby had for years, so it was possible.

And Brit was willing to do a lot for that kind of peace.

KIRBY

Kirby picked a spot in the bathroom to lay down the plastic, so she could dye her hair. She'd done this so many times, she knew what to protect, how to get even coverage on her hair, and how to get rid of the stench of the dye when she was done. She even had a subtle plan to dispose of everything when she was done, so it wouldn't be linked back to her room.

Going through each step helped her slide into a mechanical state of mind. It let her block out her emotion and follow a list. It was cool and calm in that mental place.

Until she had to pause, to let the dye set for thirty minutes. Her mind drifted toward Brit. Toward the last time they'd seen each other. Toward the betrayal and Kirby's spiral into darkness after.

She couldn't tumble into that place. Even teetering on the edge clenched her lungs and flooded her thought with inky sludge. If she fell in, she might not climb out again.

Kirby knew this sensation. It had been a long time since she felt it so strongly. It was the crash she always got after the pain. When she'd learned to cut for the high. Before Starkad showed her—

She couldn't go down that road of thought. She turned on the TV, and flipped through the channels until she landed on historical footage from World War II. Shouting at the screen about what they got wrong, and nodding with satisfaction when they had their facts right, gave her a new place to focus.

Not so much that she didn't glance at the clock every few seconds, waiting for her time to be up. Ammonia burned her sinuses and stung her eyes. Focusing on the discomfort helped ground her.

She rinsed out the dye until the water ran clear. The dark swirl ran down the drain. Spiraling like she'd done years ago. Falling. Drowning.

She jerked her attention away from the tub. Clean up first, and then she could take an actual shower. Each task was something else she had to do with complete precision. No traces of her home-done dye-job could be left behind. That required her to concentrate on the task. Good.

Kirby finished and stepped into the shower. As the first drops of water struck her skin, something inside snapped. A thick lump rose in her throat, forcing out a sob.

She couldn't give into this sensation. This was because she hadn't taken time to collect herself after what happened with Starkad. It was a crash, and it would amplify everything that haunted her.

Tumbling into the past was a bad idea. But she couldn't stop it. The hot water erased her boundaries and drew out the tears. They flowed freely down her cheeks. She shook as she tried to hold everything back, until her legs refused to support her.

It was too much. She sank to the floor of the tub, as reality and the harsh drop of coming down from intense sex overtook her. She pulled her knees to her chest and bawled until her throat was raw and her eyes burned. It still wasn't enough.

How long since she last cried? A decade? More? She'd resisted when Starkad broke her ankle. Refused when Brit made her accusations. Was too numb when Kirby tried to take her own life.

Had she gotten weaker overnight? Did seeing Brit do this to her? Was it because she finally got what she wanted from Starkad, and it ended in the worst possible way? Was Kirby finally cracking?

She didn't care about Starkad's resisting her advances or his denying interest. She definitely didn't have complaints about the sex—it was... amazing.

None of it mattered. Not after his words. *This isn't what I wanted. Not like this*. His voice crept into her thoughts, and then picked up on a rapid repeat, taunting her. She didn't want to be his regret or mistake. She never wanted to be something he wished he could undo.

And now she was.

...not like this... He'd been thinking about them. About having sex with her. It had been more than just a passing consideration. He had expectations.

Part of her already knew, but to hear him admit it, and have it wrapped up in that tone, in that look of pity in his eyes…. She didn't know how to cope.

She cried until she couldn't anymore. Until her stomach hurt and her head throbbed. Then she forced herself to breathe once. Twice. Again and again.

This was almost cleansing. Like she'd wept out the blackness in her soul. Not that she could ever really do that. But she could survive whatever life threw at her next. She couldn't take back her mistake, but if Starkad didn't want things to be physical between them, it was about time she got the fucking hint. She wouldn't make a big deal out of what happened.

Or what he said after.

The reminder threatened to undo her again until she shoved it into the same box she kept thoughts of Brit in, and tucked it on a shelf in the back of her mind.

It was time for Kirby to go back to being the professional she was trained as. Time to stop fucking around. She had a job to do.

An empty pit in her chest, the spot that held everything she'd just cried out, wanted her to approach this differently. A tiny voice begged for her to not brush any of her feelings under the rug.

She had to. It was the only way to stay safe and sane.

An image flashed through her mind like a strobe light. It pinged in her chest with a new sensation. What was that? It floated just out of reach. She grabbed for the thought, to bring it back. To examine it.

It was Starkad. He was naked, and so was Kirby. They'd never been together like this. She closed her eyes, to will away the odd fantasy, but it grew more potent. She felt whispers of straw against her bare skin. Happiness flitted through her veins. He was smiling at her, and the warmth of it flowed through her entire body.

She shook her head violently, to force the image aside. Fantasizing about Starkad in some alternate reality was the last thing she needed to do.

But the joy that came with the images had wiped away the shadows in her mind. A fist no longer clenched around her lungs.

Kirby finished dressing and headed back to Starkad's room.

He opened the door before she knocked. "We need to talk about what happened." Traces of sadness lingered in his words.

"We've already covered the highlights." She was cool. She was professional. "We can't take it back, but we can move on." Years of training helped her pretend the mechanical response was what she wanted.

He frowned, and seconds ticked away before he responded. "All right."

Did she expect him to argue? No. She was tired of arguing with him. The sooner things went back to status quo, the better.

Another image flashed through her mind. One of those damned her-and-Starkad-naked things. She was riding him. His hands roamed her body. They were laughing. Happiness surged inside, until it threatened to burst out of her. It was the exact opposite of what they'd done a couple of hours ago.

And a childish fantasy, for her to bury.

"You need to know something else." Starkad's voice helped ground her.

"Yes, I do. How did you know where to find me this morning?"

He turned away. "I wasn't there for you." He took his seat at the desk. "I was there for Min."

What? Shock and confusion raced through her. "Why?"

"He's one of us. Works for the organization. He helps put the targets you save into protective custody. Builds them a new life."

That was awfully sweet of the god. A wash of something potent threatened to overwhelm her. Starkad had never talked about anyone on the inside by name before. He and Kirby agreed it was safest that way. So why did it feel like his keeping Min's identity from her was a betrayal? "Did he know who I was?" Last night. When he approached her.

"Yes." Starkad grimaced.

It was definitely betrayal, spilling inside. She moved further into the room but kept her distance from Starkad. She crossed her arms. "Why didn't he tell me?"

"His reasons are his own. Best I can do is guess."

"Then do that." Kirby poured her emotion into her retort.

"He saw a stunning woman who flirted back, and he was more interested in getting to know you on that level than on talking business. Same reason you were in the bar." Starkad studied his fingers when he spoke. He was keeping something from her.

Fuck him. But not literally, because live and learn. He had a point, though. If Kirby had known who Min was, would she have tipped her hand? Then again, that meant she had no idea he'd been lying to her, and concern mingled with the bitter flavors churning inside. "So he also knows I gave him a fake name."

"Yes." A smile whispered across Starkad's face. An appreciation that at least she was cautious?

If they were laying out names, Kirby wanted another one. "Who's your TOM contact?"

Starkad clamped his jaw shut.

"It's Brit." Kirby wasn't asking. Everything rushed in at once. Hurt. Betrayal. All of the emotions she'd been fighting since she found that AUG. And the clawing darkness was back too. She'd been seeking revenge for years, based on hints from the woman who had her cast out.

"I never told her you were alive. She was a source of information. Nothing more."

Kirby heard Starkad's sincerity. That didn't mean she had to like the situation. "There was a time when I would've chosen death over hearing that you were working with her. Regardless of your reasons."

He finally met her gaze. The hard mask he usually wore was as fractured as her thoughts. Sympathy and sadness shone through. "I know. And I'm glad you've moved past that."

But had she really? She wasn't so certain. "Does that mean you won't help me find her?"

"I'll do whatever you ask. I'm telling you all of this because she wants out."

"Bullshit," Kirby spat. "You don't get to dump all of this on me, and then shoulder me with the burden of her freedom. She doesn't deserve *out*."

"I could have kept this all from you instead. Which would you prefer?"

It was a bit late to ask that now. "That you make the decision, so I can hate you for it, regardless of which direction you go."

"That would make things easier." Starkad sighed. "Brit doesn't mean anything to me, outside of what she is to you. She was a student. She almost destroyed you. For the latter, I'd see her suffer. Ultimately, she tried to decide your fate, and this is your chance to do the same." He pulled out a second chair and gestured.

Kirby sat on the edge of the bed instead. "I don't know what to pick." The answer should be simple. Let Brit suffer. Keep her on the inside. Why didn't Kirby say that? Because she'd hated life on the inside. She couldn't be the only one. And because part of her still loved Brit, despite the betrayal.

It was the same self-destructive part of her that said it was smart to fuck random gods without protection. And by protection, she meant a rocket launcher.

"I don't expect you to have answers right now," Starkad said.

Good. Because his demanding a decision wouldn't make it any easier for Kirby to make one. She couldn't think with him watching her. But she couldn't drag her feet, either. "Did you know she would be here?"

"No. She told me it would be a team. She never gives me names."

"Who's her spotter?" Did it matter? Kind of a lot, yeah. Because Kirby had a feeling she knew the answer, and she wasn't going to like it.

"I don't kn—"

Kirby raised an eyebrow. She'd forgiven the half-truths up to this point, but wouldn't tolerate an outright lie.

"Mark."

She punched the mattress as hard as she could, hammering the springs and fabric until her arm throbbed in protest. Brit. And Mark. Of all the bullshit fucking pair-ups... Teams didn't have the final say in their creation, but paring snipers with people they clashed with made the trust harder and the missions more prone to error.

The flash of anger and disbelief that came with this new knowledge almost made Kirby say *kill her*. She swallowed the impulse, because for some fucking reason, she still wasn't certain.

"I can give you two days to decide," Starkad said. "Brit has a dislocated shoulder and ruptured eardrum, according to her. They're staying in town. My guess is the only reason they can do that is because she told Mark they needed to find you." Protocol dictated TOM assassins never stuck around after a job—successful or otherwise. If another attempt was needed, it was safer to regroup, than risk blowing their cover.

"Or she's playing you, and all of it is bullshit except the finding me part."

"That's also a distinct possibility."

Why did life have to be all secrets and second-guessing? "If that's what she's doing, I'll eviscerate them both." No clean gunshots. She was going to look Brit in the eye and gut her.

"And if she really wants out?"

Kirby didn't know. "I need to think. I need air."

"Where do you want to go?" Starkad was on his feet in an instant.

"Somewhere you're not." Because, so help her, she couldn't have him by her side. His presence was clouding her thoughts, and as much as she wanted to forget it, flashes of sex—both what happened and the bizarre fantasies—still teased her.

How fucked up was she, that she was fantasizing about getting laid, while discussing whether to save or execute her former lover?

Chapter Eighteen

Now

Gwydion

Gwydion stepped from the shower, humming a random tune. Last night was amazing. Seeing Kirby. Being with her. Things were back on track and right again. Finally.

Though, what the hell was going on between her and Starkad? The instant the two were in the room together, sparks almost lit the air on fire. But not the happy kind. Starkad had kept his hands to himself the entire time Kirby was in his care with TOM, but her…

She was completely smitten with her *instructor*. The affection and adoration that burned in her eyes when she looked at him were as potent as in any other life, after she got her memories back. Gwydion could see why she'd been willing to be cursed for Starkad, all those years ago.

Min lounged on his bed, still naked. Gwydion was grateful he didn't have any insecurities about penis size.

The two had been traveling and living together off and on for several decades. More on than off, since the last time they found Kirby. The silence in the room was comfortable these days.

Gwydion's phone rang, and he snagged it from its spot on the nightstand. It was Starkad.

"Yeah," Gwydion answered.

"I need a favor."

"All right, but it's going to take me a few years. I'll be in touch." Gwydion couldn't help but joke about Starkad's hiding Kirby for so long.

Starkad's growl said he didn't appreciate the joke.

Grumpy fucking berserker. "Lighten up," Gwydion said. "What can I do for you?"

"I fucked up." That sounded bad. But since Starkad was drawing things out, it was probably more embarrassing for him than it was critical.

"Sucks to be you."

"Thanks." Sarcasm dripped from Starkad's voice. "I pissed off Kirby, and she's gone. She's least likely to kill you without hearing you out first..."

Gwydion grinned. "Yeah. That's so true."

"When you finish being smug, let me know."

"That's going to take a while." And as much fun as it was to give Starkad a hard time, Gwydion was worried about Kirby. "Any guesses where she'd go?"

There was a pause before Starkad said, "For cake. Not the grocery store variety. The more expensive the better."

"In the sweets-are-as-good-as-sex capital of the world? I'm going to need a better starting point than that." Gwydion liked a good cupcake, but he couldn't imagine giving up fucking, to have one.

"She's on foot. She's pissed off and reckless. But she's not stupid."

So… that didn't narrow it down at all. "I'll find her. When I do, I'm not saying anything nice about you on your behalf."

"I wouldn't expect anything else. And thank you." Starkad's gratitude was cut off by his disconnecting.

Min was sitting up now. "What's wrong?"

"Lover's spat."

Min rolled his eyes. "There are times I envy their passion."

"This shouldn't be one of them." Gwydion yanked on some clothes.

"I'll see you when you get back."

Min knew his presence could set off an already on-edge Kirby. He knew he didn't have to say *keep her safe*. There was a lot that didn't need to be said between him and Gwydion these days.

And despite Gwydion's flippant attitude, concern welled inside. He had to get to Kirby before death did. He couldn't lose her. Not again.

KIRBY

Kirby had no idea where she was going, but she was fully aware that Gwydion was behind her. He might be an army doctor, but he was a poor shadow. She needed someplace she could confront him but still have witnesses. Mostly because she wasn't in the mood to hide or fight.

And there was a TRAX train waiting at the stop in the middle of the street. She hopped onto a middle light-rail car, ducked below window level, and doubled back so he'd look in the other direction when he joined her.

He did exactly that, scanning the side of the train that he expected her to be on.

She stepped up behind him. "You're shit as a tail." She kept her voice low, for his ears only.

The asshole had the nerve to laugh. "Maybe I'm not worried about you seeing me back there."

"Maybe you should be. Were you waiting for me to walk through the lobby?"

"Starkad called me."

Because of course he did. She stepped in front of Gwydion, used her full body to nudge him back into an empty seat, and straddled his legs. The perfect way to get people to look the other way while she patted him down for weapons. "You're not endearing yourself to me."

"I did that last night." He shifted his weight underneath her. That was either a large caliber handgun in his pants, or he was happy to see her.

"That was sex. This is different. What have you got as a bribe this time, to get me to listen to you?"

"Chocolate cake with ganache and strawberries."

Ice spilled down her spine, mingling with memories, and she slid into the spot next to him. She should be leaving. No one knew that about her. Not even Starkad. No one but Brit.

"That's fucking creepy." Not how she should respond. Why did her mouth and heart work wrong around this man?

"And here I was, trying to tone it down." He was playful through all of this. Did he realize how close he was to getting hurt? Did he care? "I didn't mean to put an abrupt end to Round Three," he said.

"Pretty sure we'd be on Four." And now she was flirting back. It was official—she was losing her mind. "And it's not happening."

"I'd assure you I'm not carrying any weapons, but you wouldn't believe me unless you checked for yourself."

Kirby's concern should be growing with each passing moment, and instead she was relaxing. She needed to keep her head in the game. "You're not packing, because you could crush me with a single thought?"

"I'm not armed, because I hate death." His abruptly somber tone rang with vivid honesty. "And we're here."

The train had stopped. The block looked like any other downtown, but a few doors down from the station, one of the shops proclaimed *Gourmet Bakery.*

It was early afternoon, and the place was almost empty. It looked more like a diner than a bakery, with high-backed booths and laminated menus.

They ordered at the counter. Gwydion had the nerve to look surprised when she got yellow cake with bananas and whipped-cream frosting.

"I don't like strawberries and chocolate." She was lying. She adored both, or had until Brit ruined them for her.

They grabbed their food and picked a booth near the rear of the dining room. One with a full view of the place, including all doors.

Gwydion didn't complain about sitting with his back to the door. Her skin crawled at the thought of being so exposed.

She was slouched low so she could watch the front windows, but people outside shouldn't be able to see her.

"How do you know Starkad?" she asked.

"I've worked with the organization in the past."

Funny how Starkad hadn't mentioned he knew both the men she was with. "Did you know who I was last night?"

"Yes. He talks about you."

Kirby didn't know what to do with that information. Starkad shouldn't be telling anyone about her. But there was a childish, stupid part of her, swooning because *he talks about me?*

"I highly doubt your name is something he goes around broadcasting." Gwydion picked at his cake—carrot with cream-cheese frosting. And raisins. Talk about ruining a perfectly good cake. "But he and I have a common enemy in TOM."

This conversation was putting her at ease, and that made her nervous. Everything about the setup of meeting him last night, of his following her today, was wrong. That he knew what her favorite dessert used to be and wasn't bothered by her paranoia.

Yet he was easy to talk to, and the sex… Amazing. She felt like she could be herself around him. Even the walls she kept in place with Starkad didn't want to stay up. The entire thing made her realize how tired she was of hiding herself, both inside and outside.

She didn't want to talk about TOM or the organization or killing or hunting. A longing welled inside, to have a normal conversation. That didn't mean she had to drop her guard. "Were you alive when cake was invented?" she asked.

"At least in one of its incarnations. I mean, I wasn't *there*. I was probably in China or Uruguay, or something. When was cake invented?"

"You don't know?" That was an easier response than admitting she didn't have any idea either.

"It's not an important date on my calendar." He sectioned off a forkful of his food and offered it to her.

It was familiar to lean in and take a bite, as though they'd done this dozens of times. Oh, and it was good, too. Even for something with raisins in it.

"I can tell you when Queen Victoria's favorite lady-in-waiting lost her virginity." Gwydion reached across the table and stole one of her banana slices.

She should have been angry at the assumption, but instead it made her smile. "Was it to you?"

"No, though she claimed it was. And I can tell you when John Smith's birthday is."

"Who?" She didn't know that name, aside from it belonging to half the population.

Gwydion smiled. "No one you'd know. I served with him in the US Civil War. He was a great guy."

"So you fought for the North?" It struck her as funny. For most people, talking to a guy about being alive more than a thousand years would be surreal. Given her upbringing, this was as normal as a conversation could be. It was wonderful.

"What makes you think I didn't wear gray?"

She shoveled more cake into her mouth. It was really good. "You didn't call it the War of Northern Aggression." A vivid image flashed through her mind. She was naked. Again. But this time, she was with Gwydion. Cotton bit into her bare skin, and grass poked through the fabric instead of straw. The foul stench of horse shit and blood interrupted the fragrant scent of the bakery, and then vanished again. But a puff of joy lingered in her heart, like it had earlier. They were by a fire, close enough to the flames and each other to stay warm, despite the chill in the air.

It was as if she'd lived that moment. The taste of the air almost overwhelmed her food.

She took a giant swig of iced coffee, to wash the weird flavor away, and forced herself to stay in the now. "How many young maidens have you deflowered over the centuries? Or do you call them virgin sacrifices?"

"I don't keep track. And you don't want to hear about that."

Part of her wanted to hear it, specifically to prove to herself he had flaws. "I might. Maybe I have kinky fantasies about watching a hot guy with another woman. I'd let you watch me with another woman."

Another scene flashed in her thoughts, like a fully-immersive movie. It was potent. Stronger than the underlying memory of being with Brit.

"Noted. I'll make a list, so I can take you up on a fantasy or two in the future." Gwydion's response helped keep her here.

It was going to be a long list. The thought echoed in Kirby's head on a strong thread of déjà vu, and she shook it away. "You assume there's going to be a future."

"I'm kind of arrogant like that."

She shook her head, trying to rattle the odd imagery loose, and her gaze landed on the glass. Her gut clenched. Brit and Mark stood outside.

Please let the lighting and new hair color be hiding me. She slid under the table and came up next to Gwydion.

"What are you—"

She pressed her lips to his, silencing his question. He leaned into the kiss without protest, bringing his hands up, to cup her face. Sparks of desire raced through her, signing in her heart and stealing her breath.

When they broke apart, he didn't move away. "Are we hiding?" he murmured. "This is all sorts of Cloak and Dagger and cliché."

Like most of Kirby's life. She didn't have a witty retort, though. She was too focused on trying to keep the rage and panic from surging inside. She didn't want to taste her cake a second time. She dipped her head to Gwydion's ear, to keep up the appearance of a couple making out. "Pair just walked in. I need to leave without being seen."

And then follow them, and kill them in private.

"I've got you. I promise," he said.

And she believed him. She didn't understand why, but she trusted him to do what was needed.

A cell phone chirped, and Mark's voice reached them. "Yeah… Hang on. Let me step outside."

This was perfect. "Is he leaving?" Kirby asked.

"Yes."

"Follow him, please? And be more careful than you were with me." She hated to make the request. It would put Gwydion in danger. The only reason she was okay with him doing this was because he couldn't die.

Besides, she couldn't ignore the voice inside, telling her to confront Brit alone.

The one berating Kirby for not having made up her mind yet—about whether to kill Brit or let her survive—was louder, and she loathed herself for that weakness.

Chapter Nineteen

Brit

Brit stepped out of the line, to wait for Mark to return.

The heat that met her back cranked her adrenaline to full blast and yanked her into the past. That explained the male half of the couple, who had just walked out the door behind her spotter.

"Hello, partner," Kirby whispered in her ear, pressing into her from behind. "It's been too long."

This was familiar. Intensely close and intimate.

Brit's fingers twitched with the instinct of reaching for her gun. With her right arm in a sling, there was no way she'd get any sort of drop on Kirby. Not that she wanted to. Apology stuck in her throat. The desire to beg for forgiveness.

But self-loathing held her back. She didn't have the right.

Her body remembered this closeness, and begged her to grind back into Kirby. Phantom want mingled with her growing nausea. "You sound and feel incredible for a ghost."

"And I look much better than you do."

"Always a matter of opinion." Brit risked a look toward the front window, both at Mark talking, and to see her reflection. Apparently Kirby was a brunette now. And that asshole Mark wasn't even glancing in their direction. "How long do you think your guy can hide from Mark?"

"Not long if Mark is paying attention." Kirby dug her fingers into Brit's hip, hard enough to bruise. "He's real lousy at following people. But he's also immortal, so Mark can ditch him or cause a commotion failing to kill him. You and I will be done before then, regardless." She nudged Brit toward the back door.

Brit could almost read the strategic part of Kirby's plan. There was no reason to struggle before she had a real out, and as soon as Mark dispatched that asshole, he'd come find her. She just had to pray Kirby killed her before then.

She wasn't going down that path. She'd worked too hard to survive this long. She also wasn't going to beg for mercy or anything else. Defiance kept her cool mask in place, as they headed into an alley behind the cake shop.

The instant they were clear of people, Brit's chances of survival diminished greatly. "Sneaking away for a little one-on-one? Just like old times." Her own betrayal made the teasing taste foul.

"Not *just* like." Kirby dragged her nose along the side of Brit's neck. The feather-light touch would be enticing—it certainly called to the past—but the implied threat overrode everything else. "This time I know you're a heartless bitch and the most incredible actress in the world."

The words hurt more than the dull throb in Brit's ear. The love had been real. Not that it mattered now. "I never faked anything."

"See, I'd like to believe you, but… Actually, no. I'll never trust another word out of your mouth. Not that there will be many more."

"You're here alone." Brit wouldn't point out that Kirby could have killed her the instant they stepped out here, and walked away. The longer they stayed, the harder it would be for Kirby to do anything without getting caught.

"I'm here with the god who's trailing Mark."

"But not with Starkad."

Kirby moved her hand to Brit's injured shoulder and squeezed.

Brit had to bite the inside of her cheek, to keep from screaming in pain. There would be an advantage to drawing attention, but the downside was Brit getting caught up in the aftermath.

"He said you'd killed yourself." Hearing that from Starkad had devoured Brit. Saying it aloud now surged in her throat on a wash of bile.

"I tried. That's the last time I'll make a mistake when it comes to you." Kirby's voice was flat and cold.

"Would it help if I said I'm sorry?" That was more flippant and far more antagonizing than most of the things Brit could have said. But she was. She regretted what happened so much.

Kirby applied the faintest bit of extra pressure to Brit's bruise. *Fuck*, that hurt.

"Nothing you say is going to change anything," Kirby said. "Though, I'm dying—pun intended—to hear your beautifully tragic bullshit about why you did it."

Brit's panic was growing. Kirby should have either killed her or left—or both. And where was Mark? This was going from bad to ridiculous. "Are you serious?"

"What about this situation make you think it might be a joke?"

"I did it because you were holding me back." Even now, Brit couldn't bring herself to tell the truth. If Mark heard… Why had she let him haunt her for so long? So once again, she made the same mistake she'd made years ago. She let Mark's reality bleed into her words, and she hated herself for it.

Kirby's grip faltered, but she didn't let go. "You really believe that."

"You were always stepping between me and my potential." Brit almost choked on the words. "You kept me from growing. From becoming more. Because you were terrified someone might be better than you."

"I… I protected you. I kept you safe." Kirby sounded like she actually believed that.

Brit blinked back tears. "You suppressed me. You made me a laughing stock. The girl who couldn't stick up for herself, so she had to have her big, bad girlfriend do it for her." None of that was Kirby's fault. It was all Brit's.

"I loved you," Kirby said softly.

Once upon a time, that phrase made Brit's heart soar. Now it was another reminder of where she fucked up. "Don't say that. Please."

"You really think—" Kirby gurgled, then wheezed as she dropped her grip. Her knee landed in Brit's back, but it lacked force.

"Now, now. None of that, love," Mark said.

Brit spun, to see Mark had finally joined them. He stood behind Kirby, holding the thin, metal wire that dug into her throat. Blood seeped from the edges of the garrote.

Brit watched, horrified, as Mark tightened his grip. Kirby kicked and twisted, doing everything she could to shake him loose. His training was the same as hers, though. He'd subjected her to physical-attacks-disguised-as-training for years. He knew how to side step and keep her off-balance.

Should Brit do something? Help? Indecision warred inside. She didn't know who she would side with. As she watched the life drain from Kirby, the terrified little girl she used to be crawled back, whimpering. Telling her to not let Kirby die. Step in. Save her.

But this was Mark. He was stronger. He always had been. Brit could barely fight him on her best days.

Kirby was right. I do need protecting.

The unwelcome thought singed Brit's mind, and she shoved it aside in a silent roar of fury.

Kirby was unconscious. Then the life drained from her body, and her chest stopped moving. She was gone. Grief surged in Brit's throat. She choked it back.

Mark tossed Kirby's body and the garrote aside. Blood pooled from the neck wound.

"We need to go." Mark reached for Brit.

She needed to stay. To take responsibility. To be punished for letting this amazing woman die.

"Brit. Now." Mark grabbed her good arm and yanked her down the alley. "When we get back to the hotel, I'll have home base check traffic cams. Get online, rent us a car. We're done here."

Brit didn't take orders from him; she gave them. She was the team leader. Her protests died in her throat. Her insides were shriveling, and she couldn't stop it. She wanted to collapse on the pavement and sob. Kirby was dead.

And Brit was a shitty person, because she kept walking. Worrying about her own safety. Starkad would never help her now. Was she stuck in this life forever?

Not that it mattered. Kirby was dead. Actually gone this time.

KIRBY

Gwydion was furious with himself. He'd lost the guy he was following. Where was he? Where was Kirby?

He wandered the street. They weren't here. Where did Kirby go?

He headed toward the back of the cake shop. Kirby lay unmoving on the pavement.

His grief soared. Blood covered her chest. There was so much, he couldn't tell where it came from. He knelt next to her, searching for a wound. For a pulse. He couldn't find either.

The garrote on her chest should have been a clue, but her throat was intact.

This couldn't be happening. Not again. He couldn't keep doing this. *She* couldn't. Each death was another she had to remember in a future life. How many times did she have to lose her life, before Odin's fucking curse was satisfied?

Gwydion wasn't letting her go. He was a fucking doctor. If the blood wasn't hers, maybe she could be brought back. He'd lost Mark less than five minutes ago. How long has she been like this? It didn't matter, he was resuscitating her. He looped his fingers together and compressed her chest.

She gasped and bolted straight up.

"Holy fuck." Her voice was scratchy. She touched her chest. "Are you trying to break my fucking ribs?"

"You were…" What was he going to tell her? *Dead?* She looked fine, aside from being covered in blood.

She gingerly pressed her fingers to her throat. "This hurts too. What happened? That asshole was choking me. Did you save me? Whose blood am I wearing?" As the questions tumbled out, her voice grew stronger and more clear.

Had she died and come back? She hadn't recalled her past yet. Perhaps she hadn't been dead after all. His panic could have kept him from being rational. This wasn't the time or place to ponder it. He pulled Kirby to her feet. "Can you walk?"

"Yeah. I'm fine."

He'd question this later. "Good. We need to get you out of here now."

"I'm not going anywhere like this." She gestured to her blood-covered shirt.

Right. Fuck. She was alive, though. The reminder flooded his thoughts. "Wait here. I'll get you something to cover up with."

"Hurry." She stepped behind a dumpster.

He turned away, and impulse raced through him. He spun back to her and kissed her hard, pouring all his relief and desire into the connection.

She leaned into him with a sigh, then planted her hands on his chest and gently pushed him back. "Brit and Mark know who you are. We need to get off the street and call Starkad."

"Agreed." He was grateful one of them was thinking clearly. He headed toward a nearby souvenir shop, purchased a couple of oversized T-shirts and the first pair of pants he saw, and returned to Kirby.

"Keep an eye out," she said as she pulled a black top over what she already wore. There was no hesitation or fear in her actions.

The differences in this Kirby were more noticeable than any of the hers he'd met in the past. She was more detached. More practical. He hated it, but she was also safer this way.

They couldn't risk hopping back on public transportation. They found a motel within walking distance. Kirby seemed to close in on herself as they walked along the sidewalk, like she was hoping to vanish into the concrete.

Given the number of people who didn't give them a second glance, it seemed to be working.

Gwydion got them a room. The instant he locked the door behind them, she seemed to relax.

He wished he could do the same. He needed to know what happened. "I should examine you. Make sure you're really all right."

"Ooh, we get to play doctor?" Her teasing tone was marred by an underlying thread of tension.

Her question was a callback to their time in Kuwait. He couldn't lose himself in memories now. "Something like that."

She dumped the remaining contents of his souvenir shop purchase onto a bed, stripped everything off her upper body, and shoved it in the bag. "I'm all yours, doc. I'm fine, though."

He wished this could be an erotic, playful moment. His adrenaline was too high for him to take the thought further. "Are you?"

"No." She crossed her arms over her chest, hiding her breasts, and sank onto the edge of the bed. "I'm making countless lists in my head. We have to burn the clothes. Did I leave more than trace blood at the scene? We have to get a clean-up team in there. He got the drop on me. He never should have been able to sneak up on me. I feel like I'm falling apart from the inside-out. I don't know why I'm telling you this. I—"

"Stop." Gwydion knelt in front of her and rested a hand on her leg. He held her gaze. "Focus on me."

"You have blood on your hands. Did you leave any fingerprints? You were Army. You're in government systems—"

"Kirby." He knew she was following a panicked list of things to check for because it was easier than acknowledging what happened to her. He'd been in in her shoes. "One at a time. Are you listening?"

She clenched her jaw, but she nodded.

"I've been keeping who I am secret for more than a thousand years. They won't trace me from a random fingerprint. I'll call Starkad. You'll wash off the blood and tell me what you need, in order to get rid of the ruined clothes and any mess left in the tub."

"She stood there and watched him try to kill me." Kirby's voice was tiny. "This wasn't just her turning her back on me or lying about our relationship. She looked me in the eye, while I was dying."

He cradled her face. "We'll deal with what we can, as we can. One foot in front of the other. All right?"

"Why?"

"Why what?"

Her frown deepened. "Why are you doing all of this for me? You've saved me twice, and sure, the sex was good, but no sex is *that* good."

Because I love you. Because I fell for you the first time we met, and every time we find each other, I fall again. "Do you trust me?"

"Yes." Her answer came after a puff of hesitation.

"Why?"

This was usually where she said, *Because my heart tells me to.*

"Because Starkad does."

Gwydion would take it. As long as it kept her safe. "I don't see any wounds on you, and you're not favoring any limbs. Take a shower. We'll talk after you're clean and I've called Starkad."

Kirby stood and slogged toward the bathroom. She paused in the doorway but didn't turn around. "When you talk to him?"

"Yes?"

"Tell him this is Brit's fault. Tell him I've decided." The doubt was gone from her voice, replaced with ice and determination.

He didn't like the abrupt shift, or that he knew without asking that she was talking so casually about killing someone she'd supposedly loved. "I will."

CHAPTER TWENTY

NOW
KIRBY

There were times during Kirby's training when she went weeks without a shower. In the last couple of days, she'd used enough bathwater she was becoming part fish.

She rubbed herself dry, but the fibers of the towel felt odd against her skin. As though she was half-participating in, half-watching the moment. A similar sensation tingled in her neck.

She looked in the mirror for the gazillionth time. She didn't see anything out of place. There were no bumps or unusual ridges when she ran her hand over her throat. But there was a whisper of pain.

And there was a blank spot in her mind that she couldn't climb around or over or through, no matter the angle she approached it from. She remembered talking to Brit. Cursing herself when Mark snuck up on her. Pain.

And then waking up to Gwydion, leaning over her.

Kirby would destroy Brit and Mark for what they'd done. Now. In the past. There was no place for nostalgia or lingering shadows of affection. *You were holding me back.* Brit's voice whispered through her thoughts. *Stepping between me and my potential.*

She wrapped her towel around herself and wandered back into the main room. Doubt licked her senses. She sank onto the edge of the mattress. Brit didn't deserve a second consideration. Or third. Kirby hadn't done any of those things Brit accused her of.

If she could reach past the block in her mind... If she could see what else happened this afternoon, maybe there would be answers about why she kept hesitating to kill Brit—

She was with Starkad again, in her mind. They were naked. Or wearing wool. Or wrapped in fur in front of a flickering fire. Each texture scrubbed her skin at the same time, all of them punctuated by his touch. She smelled animals and smoke and fresh rain.

Regardless of the setting, he watched her with an adoration that reflected her own. There was no bitterness or resentment in his liquid-blue eyes. A beautiful ache spread through her chest.

The *click* of the door jarred her back to the present, and tension replaced longing for moments she'd never lived. The only weapon within reach was her towel or the clothing on the bed. She'd have to move fast and hope whoever it was didn't have a gun or hesitated to shoot.

Gwydion stepped into the room. The instant he saw her, he smiled. "Not that I'm complaining about the outfit, but I got those for you, if you'd like something that stays on better."

Another series of flashes tried to consume her, featuring him. She could almost taste the sand and traces of wine as she studied him. She refused to fall into the strange fantasies, and grabbed for the clothing instead.

Kirby dropped her towel, and Gwydion raised an eyebrow. Modesty didn't even make her list of *important* right now.

"Nothing you haven't seen, Doc. On me and I assume hundreds of other women." She tugged the shirt over her head. It said *Ski Utah* and hugged her torso tighter than she was comfortable with. Next up was a pair of knit pants with unicorns on them. "And your fashion sense is impeccable."

"I'm sorry I didn't have time to hit up Nordstrom, Your Majesty." Amusement shone on his face.

The teasing should have rubbed her wrong, especially with everything else clawing its way through her veins, but his playfulness was genuine. "At least no one is going to look at me and think *Killer*."

"At least." His smile faltered, but was back again so quickly, she might have imagined the shift. "Starkad is bringing your things. But not here."

Starkad. Her mind and body and heart were an electrical storm of confusion every time she thought about him. She'd crushed on him when he was still her instructor. Lusted after him when he saved her. Been desperate to grab his attention as anything other than *Kirby the Killer* for years.

Now there was a deep-seated ache, too. It was longing and desire and adoration and commitment. If she had any idea what love was, she might call it that. But she didn't love him. She refused to admit that was an option.

Gwydion watched her with concern and... tenderness? That whole encounter with Brit fucked with Kirby's head more than she needed. "What's with the look? Am I gonna live, Doc?" she asked.

"Yes. Definitely yes." His words didn't carry the conviction she would have liked.

Déjà vu looped in her thoughts, the brief exchange overlapping something she couldn't quite grasp. She need to focus on being present, rather than losing herself in a series of ill-timed fantasies. "What happens next?" She knew what the answer would be if she was doing the planning, and if his reply was too off base, she'd walk away from him without hesitation.

Maybe a little hesitation.

"Starkad is doing... whatever he does. He told me it would take time, and that he'd tell you but not me," Gwydion said.

That might be a lie, but it did sound like Starkad. It was also comforting, in this sea of *everyone knows and trusts everyone else.* She grabbed the remote. "You a fan of history shows?"

"I'm not. Living it once was enough."

Someone knocked.

"Besides"—Gwydion reached for the door— "you're not staying here. Min is taking you someplace safe. He'll probably watch documentaries about the Civil War with you if you ask."

That was specific. Min was another odd bit of a puzzle Kirby didn't have all the pieces for. Something about him didn't sit right with her. His name, his presence, and his hands' gliding along her skin sent shivers of pleasure and doubt up her spine. It was a flavor of fear she'd never tasted anywhere else. The most delicious flavor yet.

MIN

Min hadn't expected to set up safe houses and erase identities twice in one mission, and he'd always hoped when he set Kirby up, it would mean she was done. That she was theirs and no one else's.

He pointed her to a room in the restored Victorian in the Aves, and something new occurred to him. As she nodded her *thanks* and chose to search the house herself, the realization clutched him harder than most things had the power to these days. She wasn't getting out of this. Not intact. And never while TOM existed in its current incarnation. For centuries, he'd searched for her each time she was reborn. And in two decades, she'd become something brand new. She'd always be what she was raised to be in this life, and she wasn't the only one.

He was torn between resenting Starkad for dragging her—all of them—into this twisted game the gods played, and being grateful for the lives they'd saved. The innocents they'd snatched from misguided deities.

This was a flash in time, though. Barely a blip on the radar. If she survived… He hated thinking that way. *If.* But if she made it out alive, they'd have eternity to become more together. She'd be his queen. By his side.

"I'll stay out here for now." Kirby stopped in front of Min, back straight, almost standing at attention. Her gaze continued to flit, rather than focusing on him.

He gestured toward the living room. "You're welcome to sit."

"You first." She followed him at the edge of his peripheral vision, just out of arm's reach.

He settled on the couch.

She paced the length of the throw rug in front of him. She was like a caged panther. Graceful. Sleek. Always on alert. "I won't be sleeping for a while. I hope that's not an issue."

"Not for me. I've provided you with safety, but I don't dictate what you do."

"What if I want to leave? What if I walk out the front door right now and don't tell you where I'm going?"

The *am I a prisoner* conversation. He had this with most of the victims he relocated. While they weren't prisoners, they also couldn't safely leave, and he ensured they knew that before they made their decision. The answers for her were different. "Then that's what you do. It's my understanding you can take care of yourself. I'd be hurt. I enjoy your company."

"Which part of it? The bit where I play your toy for a couple of hours while we fuck, or when I swing in the completely opposite direction and become abrasive and confrontational?" Kirby's laugh was almost a bark. She paused and raked her fingers through her hair. "Do you ever feel like you're losing your mind?"

"Yes." *Every time you die.* Was she starting to remember, or just overwhelmed by the events of the last few days?

Gwydion believed she may have died this afternoon, but her lives had never happened this way. She didn't come back from death. Min couldn't fathom how it was possible, before she remembered who she'd been. He didn't want to get his hopes up, but this time felt different in so many ways.

"She never directly tried to kill me"—Kirby's voice was quiet, as if she were talking to herself—"but she stood by and watched twice. Not literally, the first time. Close enough. Yet there's still a part of me that longs for what we had. It wasn't even real."

"It was real to you."

Kirby let out a shaky sigh and resumed pacing. "I was an idiot." The pain in her voice and the distant look in her eyes carried so much more love and pain than a simple synopsis of her past.

"Whatever happened, you did what you thought was best at the time." Min didn't know much of the story of her past. Starkad said it was Kirby's to tell. What he'd been told was that a former lover betrayed her, that same woman wanted asylum now, and Kirby wanted her dead. "And whatever you need to do now, I support that decision."

"I need help finding and killing someone. That's what I do."

"It is."

She stared at him for a moment. "And you're okay with that? You didn't even flinch. Isn't your goal to save people?"

How best to put this? "No one is without guilt in this war. This series of battles that rages, that most of the world will never see. I chose my side, and this other woman fights against what I believe in."

"Which is… what? What does a god believe in, besides themselves?"

"Free will. The goodness of people. You."

Her chuckle faded into a frustrated sob. "You need a new list."

Min's heart cracked at her cynicism. "You don't believe in yourself?"

"I do. There are two people in this world I have faith in, and I'm one of them. But you don't know me. You shouldn't trust me. And you definitely shouldn't trust people in general."

"Who's the other one, and why?" He knew the answer, but wanted to hear her say it. He also knew it was a lost cause to follow the rest of her statement. They wouldn't change each other's minds by arguing about who was right.

"Starkad. He's done things I don't agree with—*Freya*, that's the understatement of the hour—but…" She sighed again, as she sank onto the couch next to Min and dropped her head into her hands. "In school they taught us how to act normal. *This is how you fit in. This is how you look like everyone else.* But they never actually let us *be* normal. Normal people worry about things like being late to work or if their partner is seeing someone else. If I'm late to work, someone dies. And I'm stressing about whether or not I can kill my ex before she finally offs me. I'm all over the place right now. I'm sorry."

Kirby had always been Min's Huntress. From the first life he met her in. But now she embodied the nickname in a whole new way, and her struggle with that part of herself broke his heart. "We can do whatever you'd like. Your choice."

"Such dangerous words. *Your choice.*" She grabbed the TV remote, tossed it gently in the air, and caught it. "When Brit and I had our first real mission, we were allowed to do whatever we wanted. *Finally.* No rules. No watchful eye. And we did. We watched too much TV and ate whatever we wanted. We ordered every flavor of cake on the menu. Fucked all night long—I thought it was making love at the time, but she never loved me."

"It sounds beautiful."

"It's one of the worst memories I have. It hurts to even summon it."

He wanted to wrap her up and comfort her until her world faded into the background. But that wouldn't erase what had been done. Worse, she would carry this with her for eternity, whether in this life or future ones. "Would you take those moments back?" he asked.

"The past is what it is." She was so practical, it ached.

"Hypothetically. If you could take it back, would you?" He rested a hand on her knee, to stop its bouncing.

Kirby frowned and was silent for a moment. "No. It's bittersweet, but it shaped me. I wouldn't change who I am today."

Something to be grateful for. "Would you like me to decide what we do?"

"Yes."

"La Femme Nikita?" He'd seen it a dozen times. It was Kirby's favorite movie in her last life.

Her scowl spoke volumes about her feelings on the matter. "If they get any technical details wrong, you're going to learn just how not-fun I am to watch movies with."

"I could never think that, but point taken." He took the remote from her. "Pretty Woman?"

"I've never seen it."

He queued up the film. "I think you'll enjoy it. And we won't eat cake or fuck all-night long. We'll watch this movie and the next, and enjoy each other's company until we have the next step of a plan."

The corner of her mouth tugged up, and some of the tension faded from her posture. "You make it sound simple."

"Sometimes it is."

"No. Life is never simple." Her sadness was back, heavy in her voice.

Min pulled her into his lap, and she didn't resist. "I suppose it's not," he said. "But parts of it can be." He let the movie play.

As they watched, she knew half the lines. She really was remembering her past.

"I thought you hadn't seen this." He kept his tone plain and casual.

"I haven't… Or maybe I forgot? What would it be like, to have that?" She nodded at the screen as Julia Roberts laughed and slid low in the bathtub. "I mean, everything that's making her smile right now."

"I'd give it to you if you wanted."

Kirby went rigid in his lap.

Min should be more cautious with his words. Gwydion always warned him against coming on too strong. Min had never been good at holding back, though. Each time they met again, she was frightened of him. Or rather, of what he demanded when it came to love. Even before she remembered specifically, part of her knew he wouldn't settle for half of her heart. He didn't mind seeing her with Gwydion or Starkad, but when she pledged her love to Min, he demanded she go all in, and he offered the same.

"No. I don't want that. I wonder what it would feel like, but I'm not interested in what she's doing," Kirby said.

He didn't know how to interpret her answer. "Why not?"

"Whoever I love has to be okay with my lifestyle. I might not be an assassin for the rest of my life, but I'm not ashamed of who I am, and I won't surrender my life because some fancy guy in a nice car flashes his massive wallet."

He managed to suppress his grin. Even in this, she was passionate. "I would never ask you to."

"Now the conversation is getting a little too serious for my taste." She slid from his lap to her own cushion.

"I tend to be a serious guy. Some people find that daunting."

Kirby clenched her jaw. He'd pushed too hard too fast. As long as she didn't storm from the house, that wasn't an issue. If she did choose to leave, he didn't know what he'd do.

His phone buzzed, and he grabbed it.

"Top-secret notes?" Her tone had gone flat again.

He showed her the message from Starkad that said, *We're outside*.

She stood, crossed the room in long strides, and paused a few feet back from the entryway. Her gaze flicked along the front windows. "Let them in."

Min opened the door for Starkad and Gwydion, who stepped inside quickly.

Starkad's glance at Kirby was brief, but some of the lines faded from his face. "Cute pants," he said, and set a duffel bag at her feet.

"Thank the doc." She hadn't relaxed any, but the desire that flooded the room was tangible for Min.

Aside from the brief encounter in his hotel room earlier, this was the first time in centuries all four of them had been in the same place at the same time. It should feel right, but something was still so very wrong.

Min wished he could say what it was.

CHAPTER TWENTY-ONE

6 YEARS AGO
BRIT

There were a lot of things Brit had struggled with since arriving on the TOM campus, but she was a master of keeping her emotion from her face.

She wasn't used to having to hide her excitement, though. She wasn't used to having enough for it to be worth suppressing.

As she headed toward Kirby's dorm room, it was a challenge to keep from skipping. To stop a goofy grin from spreading across her face.

"Evening, love." Mark's conversational tone sent the butterflies in her stomach plummeting to their death.

Fortunately, she already had her mask in place. The only good thing about this encounter. "Lance Corporal."

"So formal." Mark wrapped an arm around her waist and spun her to face him. "Do you call Kirby that, when she's got her face buried in your cunt? Or do you save the titles for when you're begging her to let you come?"

Bile rose in Brit's throat. She'd suspected her relationship with Kirby was one of those secrets everyone knew but no one talked about. However, if Mark was bringing it up, he wanted something. It probably wasn't sex. He took that at his pleasure. "I'm sorry—what? You're projecting again."

"Don't play these games with me. We both know better." His voice was hard, and he squeezed her hip until it ached.

Brit's heart slammed against her rib cage, but she never let it show. Mark was harsh under good circumstances. He made the word *cruel* feel like an understatement when she showed her distress. "Not sure what you're talking about. Can I do something for you? Did you want to run drills?"

He chuckled, and the lead ball that was her stomach dropped into her feet. "You can keep playing; that's fine. I'll talk, you listen," he said.

She swallowed hard and bit back a retort. If she were Kirby, she'd stand up to him. She'd throat-punch him or kick him in the balls. Instead, the same terror that had been there since she first met Mark kept her frozen in place.

He smirked. That was worse than the calm, neutral expression he'd been wearing. "Tomorrow morning, Kirby's going down."

"What are you—"

"Nothing she won't recover from. Just a little disciplinary action." Mark let go of Brit. "For everything she's done to me. To you."

She hasn't done anything wrong to me. The protest stuck in Brit's throat. Why couldn't she say something? Why couldn't she stand up for Kirby?

"You'll be there too," Mark continued. "You can stand by your girlfriend's side, or you can save your own ass."

There was no choice. She'd side with Kirby. Brit hated the hesitation weighing down the thought. "Kirby hasn't done anything wrong." She swallowed a gasp of relief that she managed the words without her voice cracking.

"Riiight… Thing is, she's their shining star. They won't make her suffer for long. A slap on the wrist. But if you stand by her side, I'll make sure you never recover. The humiliation that follows you from the hearing will be nothing compared to the hell I'll make your life. She's strong. You? You're nothing. You'll crumble so fast."

Brit wanted to protest, but she couldn't. He was right. She was a fucking coward. She'd let him bully her for years. Never stopped him. Never stepped forward. The sex whenever he demanded, the favors she could get him because she had special privileges via Kirby…

"Do you need anything else?" Her words were ice, despite the acid eating away her insides.

"Not right now. Have a lovely evening, Brit."

She wanted to sob as she strolled away, back straight and gait even. She wanted to curl up in a ball and cry.

Mark's words echoed in her thoughts when she reached Kirby's room.

Kirby could tell she was distracted, but Brit refused to open up. This was Brit's problem. She brought it on herself by being weak. By always letting someone else fight her battles. She had to deal with this herself.

She kept her mouth shut. Kirby looked concerned but didn't push. Instead, they spent the night wrapped in each other, talking, and making plans for their next trip.

Which wouldn't happen any time soon, if Mark was right.

Brit wasn't surprised when Campus Security knocked the next morning. She tried to steel herself, as she and Kirby were led to the hearing room. She listened with her jaw clamped shut, while Kirby was assaulted with accusations.

When it was Brit's turn to speak, she forced resolve through her veins. She would stand by the woman she loved. She wouldn't let Kirby go through this alone.

Brit took her spot in the hot seat.

Mark met her gaze, and a series of aches twinged through her body. Reminders of every injury he'd inflicted on her. The fractured wrist that never healed right. The punctured eardrum she hid, despite the impact it had on her physical training. The knife gouge that ran along her inner thigh that he swore had been a slip.

She clenched her toes to keep the tremor of fear from shaking her body.

She's their shining star. You're nothing. Mark's words echoed in her thoughts. And he was right. Brit was timid. She was weak. She was insignificant. Kirby would be fine. Brit might not survive. Because she didn't belong here, and someday, someone was going to figure that out.

It wouldn't be today. When Hel questioned her, Brit spilled out every self-loathing thought she had about herself and projected them on Kirby.

As Kirby glared back at her in hurt and disbelief, Brit's self-hatred took root.

When Kirby's mask slid in, Brit's world shattered. She'd saved herself, but at what cost to the woman she loved?

And still, she didn't have the courage to take it all back. Whatever came next, whatever horror awaited Brit moving forward, she deserved it.

CHAPTER TWENTY-TWO

Brit was ready to claw her way out of her skin, to get away from the chaos in her mind. Kirby was dead. Actually dead. Brit saw the body this time. It took all of her willpower to hold back the grief. This was the second time she'd lost Kirby, and there was no taking it back.

On the trip back to their hotel, it was all Brit could do to keep her emotions bottled. Speaking certainly wasn't an option. She should have told Kirby the truth. That the fault had always been Mark's. And once again, Brit had buckled under her own weakness and indecision. Now she'd lost Kirby again.

Brit bit the inside of her cheek, to keep from screaming in frustration.

The hotel-room door swung shut behind them, and Mark latched it.

"What the fuck was that?" Brit's question came out more shrilly than she wanted. "Why did you kill her?" This was a bad time to freak out. He wouldn't let her off with something as simple as death. She needed to bring her emotions under control.

"You're welcome." He kicked off his shoes.

"I'm *welcome*? Fuck you. Starkad isn't going to come to us after this." She was grasping for anything to explain her panic, and that was the best she could find.

Mark shrugged. "Who cares what he does? We stuck around here to get Kirby. We got Kirby."

She clenched her jaw, struggling to shove down her despair and grief. Being with TOM had fucked up her life in so many ways, and now he'd destroyed the one chance she had to get out. And the one woman she loved. A sob bubbled in her chest, and she swallowed hard.

"Unless you're upset because there's some other reason you want to talk to Starkad." Mark eyed her.

"Like what? To say *hi*? To catch up on old times?"

"To leave."

Brit's blood turned to ice in her veins, but she kept the reaction from her face. "Why would I leave?" Wrong response, and too late to take it back. She should have denied it and dropped the subject. Now she looked guilty.

She was, though. Guilty of so much.

"Listen. I get why this is hard for you." Mark's tone turned sympathetic.

That was worse than him pushing the lie. "You couldn't even begin to."

"Kirby's been this shadow over you for years. Everything you said to her in the alley was true, but the reality was so much worse."

She didn't like this at all.

"She did that to both of us." Mark stepped closer. "And then you thought she'd died that first time. There was no body. No closure. It's different this time. A chance to move on." He settled his foot between hers and rested a hand on her hip.

None of this was comforting. "Maybe you're right." Brit tried to keep her voice steady while she assessed her options for escape.

She was off balance, both mentally and physically, and he knew it. If he decided to be brutal…

"I have the perfect way to move past this." He glided his hand up her chest and cupped her breast through her shirt.

Brit tried to jerk away without disrupting her precarious position. Fighting him was a bad idea on a normal day. With her shoulder and ear damaged, she didn't stand a chance. "I was thinking I'd take some pills and sleep."

She didn't like the idea of sleeping in the same room as him, when he was being aggressive, but the drugs should block out most of the discomfort if he decided he wanted sex anyway.

"I can help wear you out." He twisted his foot, and she stumbled, falling back onto the bed. "I'll help you move past Kirby. I can even teach you how to stop being such a frigid bitch and show me a little gratitude." He wedged his knee between her legs and pinned her good arm above her head in a single sweep.

She was trained to get herself out of a number of physical situations, but that didn't calm her now. Her heart was lodged in her throat, and acid burned up behind it. The position he held her in kept her from doing much of anything.

Fuck.

Mark tore at her shirt. The ripping sound filled her ears, and the fabric burned her skin.

Brit wouldn't let him have this. Not now. Never again.

The single thought pushed aside her swelling anxiety, and numbness slid in. She felt like she was watching the show from outside her body, as he pressed his weight into her and dropped his free hand to her pants.

Every detail about the situation was clear and distinct. His flushed face and twisted grin. The hammering of her heart against her ribs. His still-holstered but unsecured gun. Because he was a reckless idiot, who never thought anything bad would happen to him.

Brit would have to reach across him with her bad arm, to get to his gun. She didn't care. Her body screamed in protest, as she flexed her shoulder. It was now or never. She pushed past the agony, grabbed his gun, and shot him in the chest.

He reared back with the first bullet. With the next two, he landed on his back on the ground.

A new kind of desperate immediacy spilled through her. The gunshots were too loud. Someone had heard. Multiple people, probably. She had to go.

She shoved his gun into her purse, ignoring the screaming pain in her arm. He didn't have a pulse. There should be more blood. Why wasn't there blood?

There was no time to stick around and figure it out. Brit needed to go. It was easy to strong-arm her way into the adjoining room, if she ignored the agony. From there, she blended into a panicked group of people, chatting and calling down to the front desk.

By the time she reached the lobby, she heard sirens. Must be nice to be one of the richest hotels in the city.

She lost herself in the crowds before police arrived to rope off the crime scene. As soon as they discovered Mark's body, they'd be looking for her—the cute blonde who had checked in with her now-dead *boyfriend*.

It didn't matter. She could lie low for a few hours. That was all she needed. Her mind looped mechanically through scenarios and lists of what she needed to do next in each case.

She grabbed her cellphone from her purse while she walked. As far as anyone else was concerned, she was another person on the street, gossiping about the cops surrounding the Marriott. She dialed Starkad. He should have taken her in when she asked. He should have kept Kirby safe. This was as much his fault as anyone's.

"Yeah." His tone was cool when he answered. The asshole didn't even have the good grace to sound like he was mourning.

It didn't matter. Brit was done playing his games or anyone's. It was time to end this. "Meet me. Give me an answer. Stop jerking me around."

"Fine. Three hours. I'll send you a location and a time. Be ready."

"I will." Because she didn't care what he was planning or who else he was going to have there. He could be organizing a flawless take-down, and it didn't matter. Brit was walking into the meeting, guns blazing. He had let Kirby die. So had she. Neither of them deserved to survive the night any more than Mark had.

KIRBY

Kirby didn't need to hear the other half of Starkad's conversation. She could tell from his tone, brief words, and mostly the way he watched her, who he was talking to.

"Brit?" she asked, as he pocketed his phone.

He nodded. The conversation hadn't been long enough for him to have any more information than he did earlier. His brief reply to Brit had said enough—he was giving Kirby what she wanted.

For six years, Brit's existence had hung over Kirby like a cloud. Mocking. Tormenting. Reminding her how foolish she'd been. But also constantly pointing out what she'd thought she had. Kirby had tried to tell herself she didn't care about the other woman. Spent so much time blaming

236

herself for not seeing the signs. Let it devour parts of her soul.

And now she had the chance to put a sharp end to that bit of her past.

"I didn't promise her anything but a time and a place," Starkad said. "How do you want to do this?"

Three pairs of eyes watched her. Two gods and a man she'd all-but raised to the same status, with the pedestal she sat him on. None of them would flinch if Kirby said, *Find me the perfect spot to execute her from.*

And then what? Would that close that chapter of Kirby's life? It had with her other former classmates. But they hadn't fucked her then fucked her over, and she'd looked each of them in the eye and asked them if they wanted to change.

Brit had taken the only life Kirby knew, and crashed it against the rocks. She'd stolen Kirby's choices with her lies.

And killing her wouldn't change any of that. Kirby would have to confront herself and move forward regardless. "We don't know if she's telling the truth about wanting asylum. If she comes with Mark or anyone else, I'll kill them."

"If she comes alone? If she's serious about wanting out?" Starkad asked.

"Then I don't want to know what happens to her. Either way, I'm done with her. She's out of my life forever after tonight." *Fuck*, it felt good to say that. It let Kirby admit that what she'd felt for Brit had been love. The confession surged in her chest and crushed her lungs at the same time. It might have been twisted, misinformed, or silly-little-girl love, but Kirby had loved her at the time.

And Brit had fed Kirby and Starkad information for the last few years. Whatever her reasons, the result was Kirby got to take others out of the system who would kill again and again.

"We don't know the area well enough. Where do we do this?" Starkad asked.

Min held up a finger. He left the room, and a moment later returned with a tablet, his fingers already flying across the screen. He turned the display toward Kirby and Starkad. "Here."

It was a four-story apartment complex and several images of the surrounding street. Kirby swiped through the pictures. The building offered multiple lines of sight, for her to watch and potentially shoot from. It was also a convenient series of photos.

"I own the property. They're the real-estate listings for renters," Min said, as if reading her thoughts.

"Are you going to let her stay there?" That would be stupid. Hiding in plain sight was sometimes the best option, but TOM would look for Brit here first, when she went missing.

"You don't want details." Min flipped the cover shut on the device.

"You're right. I don't."

Starkad scrubbed his face. "I don't want you up there alone."

"And I don't want you on the ground alone. I'd rather be by your side, but I need the best angle to hit anyone who comes at you," Kirby said. They'd split up before, but this was different. The odds were much higher it was a trap. Whatever transpired between them a few hours ago didn't matter. Not while they were on mission. They could argue, and she could be hurt, and he could be cold, after things were over.

"Min will be on the ground, out of sight, since he's the one who will relocate her. I'll spot." Gwydion didn't sound happy about it, but he did sound certain.

Kirby couldn't hide her surprise. He had to know what it meant. That being a spotter wasn't something just anyone could do. He did know that, right?

He gave her a crooked grin. "I'm a man of many talents. I wouldn't offer if I wasn't capable. Trust me, that's not a place I want to be. But I have your back."

And she believed that. "All right. We'll be in place before Starkad gives her a location. As in, we get in place now. She's expecting that. Any chance she'll know where we're setting up?" Kirby looked at Min.

"Did you learn about me in school?" Min's tangent confused her.

"No."

"As far as TOM is concerned, I'm not even on their radar, so they're not monitoring my properties. There are at least a dozen buildings like this in a five-mile radius. Is it possible for someone to guess where we'll be? Yes. Is it likely? No."

"Besides, she probably thinks you're dead. I did." Gwydion made a face, as if he'd tasted something foul.

That would explain the blank spot in her memory. But people didn't die then come back to life. Kirby didn't like trying to process the words, so she ignored the churning they caused in her gut. "That means she may not expect me. She is expecting something. She won't assume Starkad will come alone."

"It's like you said—if she's serious about asylum, none of these plans will make a difference," Starkad said. "If she's coming with backup, we can sit here and second-guess until we're blue in the face, but our caution is the only thing that matters. Consider this—after your light show with the grenade yesterday, the city is on high alert. TOM won't risk sending in large reinforcements that could draw attention. Hell, if she told them you're dead, she's going to have a hard time getting any backup in here."

"Unless she hasn't told them. Or they want you." Kirby had to be nothing in the grand scheme of gods' struggling to maintain their power, but Starkad had been someone at the school. The knowledge he must have taken with him…

The men exchanged a look she didn't understand, then Starkad turned back to her. "They're not sending a team like that when they come for me."

"What aren't you telling me?" And why did she feel like someone had just walked over her grave? She'd never understood that phrase until now.

He tangled his fingers with hers—something he never did, except after scenes—and held her gaze. "It's a long story. I promise you that when we're done tonight, I'll answer every question you ask me. Anything that's been off the table before, anything I've held back, I'll tell you."

That wasn't comforting. What had changed? Not that she was going to pass up the opportunity. "You're going to regret that promise."

"I regret not having done it sooner."

Invisible and icy fingers crawled up her spine, and she couldn't suppress her shudder.

Gwydion stood. "Later. We need as much time as possible to prepare."

"Let's go." Kirby wanted answers from Starkad, but not distractions before a mission. She compartmentalized her curiosity.

She rode with Min. Starkad and Gwydion took an alternate route in the other car. When they arrived, Kirby canvased as much of the area as she could in thirty minutes. The building was empty— Min was still remodeling. Kirby walked through every single room on the top two floors, cracking open the windows to different widths.

Then she picked the one with the best vantage point, to look down on Starkad from. She'd let Brit and anyone with her puzzle through whether or not Kirby's spot was that obvious.

Kirby settled in next to Gwydion. They kept conversation to the required exchange of information, but the silence between status updates was comfortable. It was odd, having two new people be part of this without hesitation or question.

Trusting them was odder. She was bothered that she did, but they wouldn't be here if Starkad had doubts about them.

And it was oddest knowing that Brit was about to be… gone. Vanished into a new life or dead.

Kirby expected a tug of grief or rage at the thought, but peace settled in, soothing her hammering pulse.

"Incoming." Gwydion's soft voice was distinct.

Kirby closed her eyes and breathed deeply. *Freya, help me to make peace among my enemies.* She looked again and pressed her eye to the scope. Until she heard otherwise, Starkad would stay in her line of sight. Gwydion's job was to tell her if Brit, or anyone else, was a long-distance threat.

"On approach from the north. Target is alone. Twenty meters out." Gwydion was good at this.

Kirby redirected her focus to his coordinates. A lump lodged in her throat when Brit's face filled her scope. She swallowed hard, banishing the past at the same time. This was a new start, regardless of what came next.

Brit's arm hung limply by her side, the splint gone. That was odd. She walked up to Starkad, close enough Kirby could see them both in the scope.

Starkad's lips moved. It would be nice to be able to read lips right now, but he could fill her in later. He looked directly at Kirby.

Fucking idiot. What was he doing?

Brit's bad arm twitched. In a single motion, she pulled a pistol from the holster at her waist and emptied the magazine into Starkad.

Rage ripped through Kirby when Starkad stumbled. *Shoot. Shoot now.* The voice screamed in her head. Or that was Gwydion? No, she was pretty sure it was her.

Pain seized her, threatening to crush her and tear her apart and burn her alive at the same time. Everything went white. The only thing in Kirby's world was agony.

Someone screamed. Was that her? Her throat was raw, but it was nothing, compared to the rest of the anguish devouring her.

And then the blinding light faded away, and Kirby was on a battlefield. Dirt and blood caked her skin and tongue. Shouts of rage filled the air. She didn't care about any of it. She was focused on Starkad, whom she cradled in her arms.

But this wasn't the Starkad she knew. He wore battered leather armor. His beard hung down past his chest, and his hair draped over her hand.

"I can't do this." The words came from her mouth, in her voice. Grief seized her, as she watched him, blood spattered on his skin and a gaping hole in his side. "I can't lose you."

It was true. Regardless of what trouble she had with Starkad, she'd watch the world burn, before she surrendered him. The love and terror that hammered in her chest hurt. Tears flowed down her cheeks. She'd never felt sadness like this. Never would again.

"Odin will be furious." Starkad's voice was weak. He wasn't speaking English, but she understood every word clearly.

"Fuck Odin. I won't serve him if it means losing you. I won't take you. Not to Valhalla. Not from the face of the earth." She leaned in and brushed her lips over his. *Live. Please. For me.* The words echoed in her head, and she poured their meaning into the kiss. She'd give up everything, even eternity, for Starkad.

The physical pain was back, tearing her from the past. Flinging her through time. Killing her again and again and again.

When the torment overwhelmed her, and blackness flooded her vision, she welcomed unconsciousness.

CHAPTER TWENTY-THREE

NOW
KIRBY

Something brushed across Kirby's face. Fingers? A cold cloth settled on her forehead. *Gwydion.*

No. That was her previous life. But that didn't make sense. She'd never lived before.

She forced her eyes open, and Starkad's face swam into view. Short hair. Clean shaven. Alive.

Her heart shattered, and a sob tore from her throat, as love crashed through her. It was hers, but it wasn't. She'd loved him so much it hurt. Love shouldn't cause this kind of pain.

"Why?" she croaked.

He frowned and kissed her forehead. She didn't hear his answer. Unconsciousness consumed her again.

Kirby flitted through times and places she'd never been. The pain was still there, but it was tempered by sex and passion and love so intense it made her gasp at the lack of reason behind it. She'd lived all these lives. She knew, because in most, Starkad or Gwydion or Min told her so.

This wasn't her. These women lived for hope. They thought they had a future. They were all wrong. Time and time again, she felt life ripped away in agony.

Then she lived it all again. Meeting Min for the first time. Balking as he demanded that if she loved him, she do so without reservation. Falling regardless, into nights of submitting to him and days of him worshiping her.

Then Gwydion. Always comforting. Always able to push aside her reason. Always introducing her to wild sex and insanely beautiful cities.

And Starkad. In the few lives where she found him, she'd died before she remembered. Before the memory of her first life pointed out he was immortal thanks to her. But she fell into his arms without reservation each time. Who she was now shriveled away from the intensity of their love. It wasn't fair.

Kirby couldn't stay in these fantasies—memories? With a force of will she thought she'd lost, she clawed her way back to consciousness. When she woke again, Starkad still sat by her side.

There were so many images in her head that vied for attention, but one plowed its way to the front of her mind. A memory from this life. Of waking up after she tried to kill herself, with him watching over her, begging any god who would listen, for her to survive.

"Do you remember?" he asked.

She nodded.

"It's probably a blur," he said quietly. "Take it slowly. It will all come together with time."

She didn't care about the kaleidoscope in her mind. "I thought Brit killed you."

"It takes more than a few bullets to the head and chest to take me down." His laugh was weak.

The scene from the battlefield filled her head again, so potent that the tang of copper flooded her mouth. "Thanks to me."

"Thanks to you."

Her entire body hurt, but the pain was a ghost. None of the wounds were fresh, but her training in ignoring discomfort was the only thing keeping her sane.

"Tell me what you need." Starkad was still watching her, with those warm, blue eyes. With that fucking look she'd wanted for so many years. One that didn't belong to her, because he'd saved it for someone else who used to wear her face.

Her answer lodged in her throat. This life hadn't been easy. All the others put together were cotton candy on a summer day, compared to the last twenty-five years. Starkad had been there for so much of it, and now an overwhelming love for him bled into all of it. She couldn't reconcile the two. "Gwydion. I need Gwydion."

"All right." Hurt lined Starkad's reply, but he stood.

For some reason his compliance without question was worse than if he'd pushed back. He turned away, paused, then turned back to her.

Starkad knelt next to her and cradled her face between his hands.

Conflict raged inside, begging her to pull away. Insisting she lean in.

He searched her face. "I know I kept things from you. I have reasons, and I'll explain every single one. Some things should have gone better, some things could have gone far worse. But every single decision I made, I thought it was right at the time. I don't regret any of it. *None* of it. Especially not any moments we shared. You're my Ruby, from now until eternity, and I will always love you."

The longing in her heart clung to his words, but there was too much that was bad surrounding the sensation. "I want to talk to Gwydion." She was surprised she made the request without her voice cracking.

Gwydion moved into sight.

Before Starkad could leave, another question rushed to the front of Kirby's mind. "In the other lives—the other Kirbys—I didn't meet any of you until I was in my twenties. Do you always find me when I'm younger, and wait?"

Starkad shook his head. "This is the first time… We look for you. You tend to be drawn to war and battlegrounds in each life. But we've never found you because we said *this is where she'll be.*"

She didn't like the next question that slid into her thoughts, but she had to know. "Why didn't I meet Gwydion or Min until two days ago?"

Starkad clenched his jaw.

Now betrayal mingled with pain and confusion. She turned to Gwydion. "Tell me. Why did you let them raise me in that place? Why, if you spent lifetimes looking for me, has it taken so long for me to meet you in this one?"

He glanced at Starkad, who stared at the wall, then looked at Kirby again. "They didn't think it was a good idea. Especially with me. You remember faster when I'm around you. You were a child. We wanted to protect you. Starkad didn't want me... What was the word he used?" Anger flashed across Gwydion's face. "Grooming you."

Disbelief joined the bitter cocktail of her emotions, amplifying everything instead of muting it. "Oh, gods forbid that happen." She let the sarcasm bleed into her words. "*Kirby, don't ever let them see you're weak. Kirby, pain is worse than showing someone you love them. Kirby, let me pretend to save you, only to drive home over and over and over again how unfuckable you are.* But no, I wasn't groomed."

"I did—"

"What you thought was best at the time," Kirby cut Starkad off. "*Holy fuck*, if you tell me that again... I'm not sure what I'm going to do, but as soon as I figure out what I'm capable of, it'll be bad. Get. Out."

Starkad walked out.

The images flooded back in a chaotic jumble. Those of her last life were the most potent. When her memories came back, she'd wandered out of a hotel in Kuwait in a haze of confusion. She wouldn't do something so careless again, but she needed something to tap this rush and help relieve the pressure.

Gwydion settled on the bed next to her. It was easy to shift to rest her head on his leg. She felt so weak. So pathetic. Her world was crumbling, and once again, she was doing a shitty job of dealing with it.

"Don't." Gwydion's reprimand was quiet.

Kirby didn't understand. She started to sit. He didn't want her here?

He pulled her back down. "I don't mean that. I always want you in my arms."

"Don't what?" She settled closer, needing the contact to ground herself. Would she drown in her own mind if he wasn't here?

He trailed his fingers through her hair. "Whatever you're thinking, don't. Whether it's despair or self-loathing or anything negative, don't fall down that pit. None of this is your fault. None of this makes you weak. Nothing good comes from losing yourself in a tirade of *what ifs*."

"Speaking from experience?"

"So much of it."

"I don't know what to say or where to start or how to move forward."

"You don't have to figure it out right now," Gwydion said. "You have time to process. I'm here, and so is whomever else you ask for."

She couldn't completely silence the voices of self-loathing. They were part of her. But his touch, his scent, his familiarity—it was all comforting. If she followed the line of his fingers, as he drew them along her scalp, she could almost sort some of the brain mess into the same rows.

The flashes of the past were already fading into something that didn't pollute her senses so strongly. If she stopped trying to focus, a lot of the pieces tumbled into a semblance of order. She could identify some of the strays by their setting. The clothing worn.

And then there was Gwydion. "I remember the first time one of them met you." Or was it her, in a past life? She didn't know. Those women didn't feel like her, though. She had their pasts, but not their personalities.

"In France?"

"In Wales," Kirby said. Was he testing her? "I …" She strained for the memory. "Lived on a pig farm? Really? A farmer's daughter sleeping with the silver-tongued wanderer? Fucking cliché."

"*Electrical engineer* wasn't a career choice at the time." He chuckled.

More images assaulted her. Of painted warriors, screaming through the forest, wielding spears. "It was the Battle of the Trees."

"War was different then."

"Yes and no. The magic was god-made instead of man-made." That was an almost poetic statement. How lyrical of her. "After you won…"

"I was exhausted. Drunk in victory and power. And you were the most amazing creature I'd ever seen."

"Not me." Kirby wanted to both fall into and run away from the pit of longing in her heart at the memory. "Her. A different Kirby, who wore my face. I don't love any of you." Saying that was a new kind of hurt, because she was rejecting something amazing. "All of the others did. I feel what they felt. But I don't know you. And I swear, if you tell me I *am* them…"

"I wasn't going to."

Tears pricked her eyelids. "Because I'm broken in this life."

"You're not broken. You're different. Completely unique. Parts of you resemble the other women I've loved, but I don't know you any better than you do me."

"Why are you in town? Why this job? In this city?"

"I got tired of waiting to see you."

Finally an answer that warmed her. "Are you disappointed?"

"No." He leaned in to kiss her cheek.

"I gave up eternity for him." It hurt too much to say Starkad's name.

"And he's done the same for you."

Because he'd done what he thought was best. Watched her suffer. Let her bleed. Stood back while TOM rearranged her brain and tried to make her their pet. "I don't know if I can forgive him."

"There's no rule out there saying you have to. You have a choice."

"I've had so many choices taken from me. Including by him."

Gwydion's lack of response set her teeth on edge.

"No witty comeback?" Kirby asked. She knew what he wasn't saying, though. *Starkad was doing what he thought was best.* She tried to press closer into Gwydion. Not easy, given her position, but she was going to try. She could stay like this forever. It didn't matter that he was a stranger now; her memories said he was kind and good, especially to her. And that he had some of the same cracks in his psyche that she did, from so many centuries of wars.

It was a shame the world wouldn't stop while she was in his arms. "What happened to Brit?" She hated to ask.

More silence.

"You've got a horrible poker face." Kirby sat so she could look him in the eye. "You hesitate every time you don't want to tell me the truth."

"Because I can't lie to you. She's in the other room."

Kirby's body coiled like a too tightly wound spring. "Why?"

"You... When you thought she killed Starkad, you ascended. That's where the memories came from. You also seem to have inflicted her with the memory and pain of every time you died. Leaving her behind would raise more questions than we're equipped to deal with. We can send her back to TOM or give her what she asked for, or you can still kill her."

So much for seven minutes in heaven. Kirby's rage was at the forefront again. "I want to see her."

"I don't think that's a good idea. Not yet."

"You said whatever I needed and whomever I wanted here." Kirby had to look her in the eye. She had to ask *why*, before she ended Brit's life.

Chapter Twenty-Four

Now
Kirby

Gwydion walked with Kirby down the hallway. "We could leave. You and I. They can go with us if they want, but we don't have to wait for them, in order to walk away," he said. "We could rediscover each other.

"I'm in the middle of a war." She paused a few feet back from the doorway he'd indicated.

"A war that's not yours."

She studied him for a moment. The lines of worry etched in his face. His rugged features. The stress of centuries that weighed on his posture. And he was gorgeous, in spite of and because of all of it. "If I'm a Valkyrie, this war is literally mine. And it should be yours. Mine isn't the only pantheon involved."

"They abused you. They brainwashed you. They manipulated you."

She winced with each truth. "There are things I'll never forgive them for. But I can't deny who I am. Even if I were still just plain, boring Kirby, I'd have a stake in this. With the exception of my first life, I've never made it to thirty. Fuck that bullshit. I'm going to live forever, and stopping TOM is a steppingstone toward my not dying again."

"And I don't want to discourage that," Gwydion said.

Kirby was done with his pleas. Walking away was tempting, and that was the best reason she could think of, to brush him off.

She stepped into the room.

Brit lay in bed, her skin pale and her face twisted with pain. Her eyes grew wide when she saw Kirby. "You're..." She sobbed. "Holy fuck, you're alive."

Kirby couldn't ignore the emotion in Brit's voice, but she sure as hell tried. "Surprise." She focused on Gwydion. It was easier than looking at Brit's grief and agony. "Is she hurt?" Kirby asked. Inflicted with more than a dozen deaths was painful. But Brit didn't have any visible injuries.

"Physically, she's fine, aside from the shoulder and eardrum. Those wounds aren't fresh, though."

"Can I make her stop hurting?" Kirby wasn't sure why she cared, but she did.

"You can give and take life. I don't know what you can do for pain. But you magically inflicted her wounds, so I assume you can remove them."

"Are you two actually talking like crazy people, or is it the drugs?" Brit's question was slurred.

Kirby should have anticipated that. "You drugged her."

"I'm not big on torture." Gwydion leaned against the doorframe. "She was suffering. I gave her morphine."

Kirby crossed the room and knelt next to Brit, who watched her closely. Knowledge she didn't realize she had said she didn't need touch, to inflict the pain, but she was still figuring out the extent of her power. "I want you lucid for this."

She brushed her fingers over Brit's shoulder, and healed her eardrum. Then she visualized drawing the drugs out of Brit's bloodstream. Each movement felt as natural as walking. As if Kirby had always known how to do this.

Brit's gasp carried the weight of a rush of pain.

Kirby wasn't taking away the whispers of the past yet. She was spiteful enough to not want to feel this alone. "I'm not just talking like a crazy person. It turns out I am one. I have a dozen other lives jammed into my brain."

"I don't understand." Clarity was returning to Brit's expression and words.

Kirby had one distinct memory that wasn't from this life. One piece that felt like hers, even though she'd never lived it in this body. She summoned her wings and ethereal armor.

Brit gasped.

It was a shame Kirby had such a bad angle on herself. She probably looked kickass, with black feathers growing from her shoulder blades and polished leather padding her torso and legs. "I'm a

Valkyrie. Turns out three guys have been stalking me for centuries, to keep me from dying each time I'm reborn."

Brit pushed herself into a sitting position. She tentatively flexed the fingers of her right hand. "Reincarnation isn't—"

"A thing. I know. This is a curse, courtesy of Odin. You won't believe the things I'm remembering. I don't believe them."

Brit reached out to stroke her fingers along one of Kirby's wings. Kirby resisted the desire to flinch away from her touch.

"Figures." Brit laughed bitterly.

Not the response Kirby expected. "What does?"

"The best of the best. Kirby, the golden child. Of course you're the last Valkyrie on the planet. *Fuck*, you're a real-life Mary Sue."

Kirby let the wings fade and didn't try to suppress the rage that flowed through her. "My life hasn't been any easier than yours. I've earned everything I have, and I've lost more than you'll ever realize." When she spoke, her voice reverberated off the walls.

"Oh boo-hoo." Brit's curtness didn't match her startled look. "If you're going to play the martyr card, just torture and kill me. That'll be less painful than you insisting you're nothing special."

Kirby could retort. She could act out in anger or vengeance. She needed to remember she was done with this. With Brit. Kirby could love what they'd had, and still loathe the woman in front of her. She pressed her lips to Brit's forehead and focused. In her mind, she saw the threads of her own memories running through Brit's body. She tugged and drew them back into herself.

Brit gasped again, this time with relief. Pink tinged her skin.

"You can go now," Kirby undid the restraints holding Brit to the bed and stepped away from her.

"What?"

"Buh-bye. Fuck you. Have a nice life."

Brit stood. Fear crept into her expression. "I asked for help."

"You got help. I didn't kill you."

"If you send me out there like this, it's as good as killing me."

That was an interesting point. Kind of like the *if you kill a killer, there are no fewer killers in the world* argument. But Kirby had confronted that demon years ago. "I survived."

"You had Starkad. A support system. You're a fucking Valkyrie. I had torture."

Was this the bullshit about Kirby holding her back again? The crawling under Kirby's skin said it was more, but she refused to get sucked into Brit's stories. "I wasn't a Valkyrie until a few hours ago, when you tried to take him from me. Just like you tried to steal my life. You don't like freedom as an option? Go back to TOM and Mark. Or did you burn that bridge?"

"If you're going to send me back to them, kill me now." Bitterness flowed from Brit's voice. "I've put up with the torture, the manipulation, and the assault for years. I'm done pretending it was anything else. I'm done hiding it from myself or caring what you think. I'm just done."

The words stalled in Kirby's mind as she tried to sort through their meaning. A series of retorts raced to the tip of her tongue, and she swallowed them all. *Why didn't you say anything before now?* Kirby never had. *Mark said I was the only one.* Because she believed that? It seemed so naïve now.

"That was the point. You already thought I needed protecting from everything. I wasn't going to give you one more reason to look down on me."

And now they were back to this. "I never—"

"It doesn't matter anymore. I killed him." Brit said with a lot less enthusiasm than Kirby would have.

The news was a little disappointing. Kirby wanted that pleasure herself. It also set warning bells chiming in her head. If Mark was dead, something was wrong. She wanted to finish the conversation with Brit, but more important things were at stake. "When? Where did you kill him? How?"

"In our hotel room. Right before I called Starkad. Mark killed you—I thought—and then he forced himself on me. I shot him and left."

This was all wrong. "*Starkad. Min.*" Kirby shouted. She kept her attention on Brit. "Are you certain he's dead?"

"I shot him in the chest three times, at less than a foot. He wasn't breathing. He didn't have a pulse. I know what dead looks like." Except Brit didn't sound so certain anymore.

"What's wrong?" Starkad asked. He and Min joined them, and stood next to Gwydion.

Kirby glanced over her shoulder. "Is the news talking about a body found in a hotel? Are the police? Is anyone?"

"There were shots fired downtown, but no one was hurt. They haven't located the gunman," Min said.

Because she was standing in front of Kirby, looking defeated and terrified.

"How much did he bleed?" Kirby demanded to know.

"What?"

Kirby was going to smack her if she asked that too many more times. "Answer the fucking question."

"I don't… I don't remember. I was panicked. I was grief-stricken. I thought you were dead."

Kirby hated that the sentiment pinged in her chest with longing. "Nice of you to finally care. I've killed sixteen of your counterparts. Face to face. You bleed the same as anyone. Was. There. Blood?"

Brit hesitated.

"Fucker's not dead." Kirby turned toward the men. "We need to go *now*."

"Grab anything personal. Clothes. Laptops. Weapons." Starkad barked orders, and no one argued. "Five minutes, and we're ghosts."

Kirby was impressed everyone moved quickly and without question. As the three men combed the house, she could see how much they'd come together in their time without her, looking for a woman she couldn't imagine ever being.

"What about me?" Brit stood behind her.

Glass shattered in the living room. Kirby's instinct kicked in, and her wings and armor were back. She threw herself over Brit.

Darkness engulfed the house.

Thank you for following Kirby through her stuttered past.

Now that Kirby's remembered who she is, someone will pay for this life and all those she's lived before. But will it be the gods, or Kirby herself who suffers? Find out what darkness awaits her and her harem, in DEATH IN THE NIGHT.

ACKNOWLEDGEMENTS

Extra huge thank you to Sotia. She's a brilliant editor, brainstorming partner, and friend. None of this would happen without her. And to Shannon, Athena, and Julie for being sounding boards, helping me talk through story problems, and reading my early, messy work. A writer with a scrambled brain isn't a pretty thing, and they take my messages regardless.

Special nod to Annette for helping me name my villains' secret organization.

Thank you to everyone who's accompanying me on this amazing journey of bleeding my imagination onto the page. My readers, friends, and especially my spouse.